Also by David Mammina:
The Circle Stone Group
(The Beginning)
The first of the Circle Stone Trilogy

The Circle Stone Group

The Other Warriors
The second of the Circle Stone Trilogy

By: David Mammina

Order this book online at www.trafford.com
or email orders@trafford.com

Most Trafford titles are also available at major online book retailers.

Printed in the United States of America.

ISBN: 978-1-4669-3436-8 (sc)
ISBN: 978-1-4669-3437-5 (e)

Trafford rev. 05/11/2012

 www.trafford.com

North America & international
toll-free: 1 888 232 4444 (USA & Canada)
phone: 250 383 6864 ♦ fax: 812 355 4082

For My Family

~The Warriors of Laven~

Sio:
Lenna – Power over nature
Chaily – Swordsman
Ursa and Vicky – Conjurors
Dimi – Multi-weapon knife
Ellia – Fighter
Ruller – Magic

Shenny – Knives
Sensho – Doctor
Grev – Spear
Meemee – Bombs

Ixie:
Divy – Power over water
Lisha – Power over fire
Mira – Power over air
Kita – Power over earth
Ery – Power over empty space

Paro:
Luc – Snake
Vesa – Fish
Feo – Bird

Helite:
Maura – Shapeshifter
Kit – Object changer
Maia – Invisibility and portal opener

Cumber:
Rui – Energy staff and flight

Table of Contents

Chapter 1:
Ixie

A small wooden boat drifted onto the sunlit coast of a small beach. The sound of the boat against the rocks on the shore awoke the girl sleeping on the deck. She sat upright, her long, red hair askew, and held her head tightly. She had a massive headache, and as she sat under her blanket, a flashback of a vicious storm appeared in her mind. As lightning flashed, wind blew, and rain poured upon her she had become overwhelmed, and she remembered hiding in a corner, waiting for the calm of the storm to come. Lenna was not capable of controlling the storm, and it had gotten the better of her.

Ever since then Lenna had been extremely tired, and she was not surprised by her pounding headache. She removed her headband and ran her fingers through her hair, trying to straighten it out.

"I should have brought a brush," she said to herself. She held her headband in her hand and looked at the six red gems attached to it. She longed to use the gems to communicate with her friends at home, but she had promised them that she would only use them in case of emergency. It had been about eight weeks since she left.

She put the headband on her head and climbed out of the boat and onto the rocky shore. Her mission, to find the warriors of this island, Ixie, and bring them back to Sio with her, would require help from the natives here. She was looking for a boy with wings and a large staff, a snake with large fangs, a girl who moved something red around, or a tree with only two branches. With such vague details, she had no idea where to begin. She began to walk.

Lenna was not entirely sure if this even was Ixie. After all, she only had an idea of its location, and even though she had stayed on course for the whole trip, she was still worried that she was not in the correct place. There were various trees scattered beside the beach, and so she walked to what she thought was the tallest one and began to climb. When she reached the highest branch which would hold her, she looked out. It turned out that the island was very small; smaller than Sio, and she could see that the opposite side of the island was only a few miles away.

The beach ran along the entire perimeter of the circular island, and the inside edge of the beach was lined with trees. Inside the circle of trees was a large village filling in almost all of the remaining space of the island, so naturally this must be where the people of the island lived. Lenna jumped from the tree branch. As she fell to the ground she spun around, moving the air around her. The air supported her, and she gracefully landed on her feet. She began to run towards the village. When she arrived, she addressed the first person who she saw.

"Excuse me," she called. The man she had approached looked at her nervously. He had lightly tanned skin and short, dark hair, the complete opposite of her fair skin and red hair. "This island, is it Ixie?"

"Yes," the man replied. "Who are you?"

"I'm just a traveler, thank you!" Lenna said, hurrying off and leaving the now puzzled man behind her.

Lenna spent the day exploring the island, keeping her eyes open for anyone or anything which resembled what she was looking for. She started in the trees, looking carefully at each one, but none of them had only two branches. Wildlife was practically nonexistent on the island, so there was no sign of any snakes, either. By the time she had walked the perimeter it was past midday, and she spent the rest of the day in the large village. She was lucky to find a small store which sold fish, but because of her lack of money, she walked out with hardly enough to eat.

Lenna hoped that she would identify one of the people in the village as the warrior she was looking for. Of course, the boy with wings would have stood out if she saw him, but he was nowhere to be found. She also passed dozens of girls, but none

2

of them were moving something red. Tired and hungry, Lenna returned to her boat. She opened up her bag of food and found that she was down to her last piece of bread and a small piece of meat. She ate it quickly with the fish which she bought in the town and laid down to rest as the sun set on the horizon.

*   *   *

There was a splash of water over the side of her boat. Lenna quickly awoke and looked around.

"Hello?" she called. There was no answer. Something moved behind her. She turned, but saw nothing but darkness. "Who's there?" she asked, her voice shaking. The only sound around her was the sound of the waves. The water was very high that night, and it was rising quickly. Before she knew it, water began to pour over the sides of her boat and onto the deck. Suddenly, a huge wave appeared over the opposite side. Lenna raised her hands and pushed them towards the wave, but the water did not stop. She was sent flying back, drenched. She fell on the deck of her boat, gasping for breath. Everything around her was becoming cold. The water on her skin was turning to ice, and she was pinned down. Finally, a voice came from the darkness.

"Who are you?" it asked. It sounded like a boy.

"My name is Lenna. I come from Sio."

"Why?"

"I'm looking for ... someone," she replied.

"Who?" The ice on her body was slowly creeping up her chest and around her neck.

"Someone ... with powers," she replied. She had to begin to explain her mission, or she feared that she may freeze here.

"What kind of powers?" the boy asked.

"I'm not sure. It could be boy with wings and a staff, a tree with two branches, a snake with large fangs, or a girl who can move something red around."

There was silence for a moment. "What do you know about the girl?" the boy asked.

"Nothing," Lenna said. She thought for a moment and then said "Oh, she wears her hair in a ponytail." There was a pause.

"Can you control water?" the boy asked.

"What?" Lenna asked, confused. How did he know?

"When I made the wave, you stopped it for a moment. You may not have noticed, but you did. What's your power?"

"I control nature," Lenna said. "Every part of it."

"And is ice not a part of nature?" the boy asked. "Let's see you get out of that," he said. His profile appeared in the darkness, advancing towards her. He sat down, waiting.

Lenna closed her eyes. She focused her mind, trying to melt the ice, but she couldn't do it without moving. Her head began to hurt.

"Stop," the boy said. The ice around her turned to water and she was soaked again for a moment. Then the water rose from her clothes, skin, and hair and jumped back into the ocean. She saw the profile of the boy's hand reaching down to her. "I'm Divy," he said. She grasped his hand and stood up.

"Why did you attack me?" Lenna asked.

"You spent the entire day walking around this island and only spoke to one person. Two, if you count the person you bought food from. If that doesn't scream suspicious, I don't know what does," he said.

"You followed me all day?"

"It wasn't difficult, you're not very perceptive," Divy answered. "But there's potential. You melted the ice."

"I didn't melt the ice," Lenna said quietly.

"You did a little. You have to practice. So, are you coming?" Divy asked, jumping down from the side of the boat. Lenna followed him. They walked into the trees until they reached a small pond. "This is my entrance to the hideout. There are four others around the island, so each of my friends has their own entrance. I'll take you to them so you can fully explain yourself. I think that you'll be pleased with what you find."

"So there are five people in your group?" Lenna asked. Divy was quiet.

"Four," he answered, and he stepped toward the pond and made a sweeping motion with his hands. The water parted, revealing a small wooden door at the bottom of the pond. He ran down and opened the door. "Get in, quickly," he said. Lenna ran down and jumped through the doorway. She fell a few feet and landed on the ground. Divy jumped through as well and then closed the door. They could hear the water rushing back. "Follow me," he said, grabbing Lenna's hand to guide her through the dark hallway. After a few bends, a dim light shined in front of them, revealing a small room.

Lenna stepped into the room with Divy and was soon being stared at by three girls. Two of them were sitting together at a table. One was short and slightly overweight. Lenna thought that she was a woman anywhere between twenty and thirty years old. She had short black hair and a kind, lovely face. The girl sitting at the table with her was younger and had longer black hair. Bangs covered her forehead, and the dark hair stretched down to the top of her shoulders. She was taller than the other girl, despite her young appearance, and she wore glasses. The third girl was sitting on the ground next to a small fire. She was chubby and had thin, curly, light brown hair, and to Lenna's surprise and joy, it was held in a ponytail. Lenna turned to Divy. It was the first time she could actually see him. He was taller than the girls and had brown hair, the back of which touched his collar and the sides covered the tops of his ears. The front of his hair was flipped up in an attractive wind-blown look. He had a young, handsome face and a thin body.

"Lisha," Divy said, "this girl is looking for you." The girl sitting beside the fire stood up. She was the shortest in the room. "She knows about your power."

"Really?" Lisha asked, stepping towards Lenna. "Why?"

"Let's find out," Divy answered. He walked over to the table that the two girls were sitting at and lifted some water out of a cup. Lisha pulled a small flame out of the fire and danced it around her fingers. Red, Lenna thought. The two of them walked over to Lenna. They stood in front of her, Divy on her left and Lisha on her right.

"When were you born?" Divy asked.

"Towards the end of the fourth month on Sio," Lenna answered, confused. The small ball of water floating between Divy's hands began to swirl.

"Can you really control all of nature?" Divy asked.

"Yes," Lenna answered. Again, the ball of water swirled.

"Do you think you're in the right place right now?" said a voice from the table. The girl with the bangs had asked it.

"Yes," Lenna answered. This time, the ball of water didn't swirl. Instead, the flame flickered and died. It burst back into Lisha's palm a moment later.

"You're lying," Lisha said.

"What?" Lenna asked.

"We'll ask you again; do you think you're in the right place right now? In other words, do you think you can trust us?"

Lenna hesitated. "I'm not sure. I don't even know any of you. I'm here because I was told to come here." This time, the ball of water swirled

"Oh, stop all of this," said the older girl. "Can't you see that you're confusing her? Your intuition's good enough, you don't need to test her." She stood and approached Lenna. "I'm sorry about them, we have to be careful about whom we let in here, but with every passing minute your face looks more and more nervous. These two love learning about people, and they just want to see what you're like."

"That's fine," Lenna said quietly, staring at this uncomfortably polite girl.

"Wait, I want to know what element she is," Divy said. "Things are different on Sio." The older girl rolled her eyes. "Oh, come on! I'm curious!" Divy looked at her and then at the girl with the bangs, who was still stationed at the table. She stood up and moved her hand towards the ground. A small pebble flew to it. With that, the older girl sighed and shrugged. The two of them walked over and stood beside the other two of their group. The older one moved her hands over each other, and the air between them became visible. Then, all four of them merged their powers together. The rock, the water, the fire, and the air became one. The rock flew out from the mix and began to circle Lenna.

"Earth!" said the girl with bangs. "You're just like me! I'm Kita!" She grabbed Lenna's hand and shook it forcefully. "I don't think we found out your name."

"Oh!" Lenna said, surprised that she didn't introduce herself in the first place. "I'm Lenna."

6

"And I'm Mira," said the older girl. "It's nice to meet you."

"Lisha, Kita, Mira, and Divy. That's easy," Lenna said, smiling. "So what was all that?"

"A test," Divy explained. "All of us can perform that first test to see if a person is telling the truth or not. Kita and I can tell when people are telling the truth, and Lisha and Mira can tell when a person is lying. When the water swirled, you were telling the truth. When you lied, the flame flickered. You need to learn to not be so unsure. *Always* tell the truth, unless you're positive that you shouldn't," he said seriously. "Now, the part about you being earth. Every person is influenced by one of four elements: water, fire, earth, or air. The element helps to decide their personality, strengths, and weaknesses. You're influenced by earth."

"So does that mean that you each control your respective elements?" Lenna asked.

"Yup!" Lisha answered. "And you can control all of nature? Wow."

"Yes, but I still can't control my powers. It's difficult."

"So why are you here?" Mira asked. Lenna hesitated. She was uneasy and felt extremely awkward. This was all happening so quickly. Divy moved across the room and took a seat, and so she followed him. The girls sat down as well.

"Have you ever been visited by Ixie?" Lenna asked.

"Ixie is a person?" Divy asked.

"No, he or she is a spirit. You see, there are four other islands in the world. Cumber, Paro, Helite, and Sio. Each was created by a spirit, like Ixie, and each spirit created warriors to defend their island. My friends and I met Sio, and he explained it all to us. My island, Sio, has been taken over by a man named Gabent. We couldn't defeat him, so four of us, myself included, set out to the other islands to find the other warriors there. We need help."

"Which basically means that you need us to leave with you," Kita said. Lenna nodded.

"How many people are there in your group?" Lisha asked. "And what can they do?"

"Well, it's more like two groups in one. The Circle Stone Group is the group that I'm in. The warriors from the original Group chose us to take their places now that they have passed away. As we tried to defeat Gabent, we made friends with four others, and they're in their own group, even though we still refer to ourselves as one group together. It's sort of confusing," Lenna explained. She turned her head toward the fire for a moment, and the gems on her headband sparkled.

"You have gems just like us," Kita noted.

"You have them?" Lenna asked, shocked. "We use them to communicate."

"So do we," Divy said. He lifted a thin, brown string out from under his shirt. It had been hanging around his neck this whole time. At the end of the necklace was a fish's tooth, and embedded in it was one gem. It was a deep blue color, yet it was different from Lenna's. She took her headband off and held it next to the tooth. Divy's gem seemed to be shimmering while hers was plain.

Kita, Mira, and Lisha had also taken out necklaces from under their shirts. They each had a fish's tooth with a gem in the middle. Kita's was a brown gem, Mira had a white gem, and Lisha had a red gem. They were all shimmering.

"Let's talk to your group!" Mira said, excitedly.

"We promised each other we wouldn't use them unless there was an emergency," Lenna said.

"Why?" Divy asked. There was silence.

"I have no idea," Lenna finally answered. "It just seemed like a good idea at the time."

"Oh," Mira said. "Well tell us about them, anyway." The four leaned toward Lenna, eager to hear about her friends.

"Okay. Well, you all know me. Then there's Chaily. He's an amazing swordsman, and one of my good friends. He's sad sometimes, though. He hasn't had that great of a life, but we won't get into that. Next is Ursa," Lenna paused. "I guess I should say Ursa and Vicky. They're twin sisters, and they're conjurors. They just grasp hands, say the name of something, and it appears! They also have these two weapons. Ursa has a chain-weight, which is like a ball on a chain, and when she throws it at someone, it can really knock them back. Vicky has this odd grappling hook that can grasp things. They're a great team, but they were split up. Vicky's in Cumber, trying to find the warriors there, while Ursa's stuck at home. After them is Dimi. He's in Paro, trying to find the warriors there. His power is sort of like Chaily's, only he uses a knife that he can change into any weapon. Then there's Ellia, who is another good friend of mine. She's a fighter and also a strong leader. She's in Sio right now. Finally, there's Ruller. He's out in Helite. He's the youngest of all of us, but he's also one of the smartest if not the smartest. He has this book of spells, and he definitely knows what he's doing. He saved us all from being killed by Gabent . . ." Lenna became silent, but quickly recovered. "And that's my group! Then there are the other four: Shenny, Sensho, Grev, and Meemee. They don't have any powers, but rely on talent alone. Shenny fights with knives, Sensho is a medicine man, Grev has a spear, and Meemee uses bombs. That's it."

There was silence in the room. Finally, Mira spoke. "That's a lot."

"Yes, and there are going to be more once the other warriors come to Sio. That is, if they will," Lenna explained, looking at the other four.

"Tell us more about Gabent," Kita said.

"Honestly, there isn't that much that I know about him. He has powers, like us, and he wants to kill us personally. He kidnapped each one of us, but luckily we were able to escape. What's good, though, is that as far as we know, he thinks that we're all dead. See, when Ruller saved us from him, Gabent would have thought that the spell he hit us with killed us. So, as long as we stay hidden, he doesn't know that we're still a thorn in his side."

"You make him sound like he's not a problem at all," Kita said.

"Oh, he is," Lenna responded. There was silence again.

"How?" Kita asked.

"Because he killed countless people as he took control of Sio and now we don't even know where the rest of the people of the island are. He hunted us from the day we received our powers and used whatever means necessary to take us. And like I said earlier, he almost killed us."

There was silence from the four from Ixie. They looked at each other for a moment. Then, Kita shrugged to Lisha who shrugged to Mira who nodded to Divy. He looked at Lenna and smiled.

"We really have nothing to do here," he said. "We're bored most of the time because we don't go out much. When do we leave?" he asked, standing up. The other three stood up with him, and Lenna looked up at them and smiled. She jumped up and embraced them all.

"Thank you so much! We'll leave tomorrow; is that good? I'll let you all have a night to rest and I'll meet back up with you here tomorrow morning!" she said. She began to walk towards the exit.

"Where are you going?" Mira asked, turning her around and pushing her back into the room.

"To my boat . . ."

"No, you're not sleeping out there. Kita," Mira ordered.

"Follow me, you'll sleep in here," Kita said. She walked over to the wall and lifted her hands. A part of the wall rose up, revealing a room with five beds and a dying fire.

"You all live in here?" Lenna asked, walking to the room. "Why not outside in the town?"

"It's a story," Lisha said. "We have a spare bed, so just sleep wherever you like." With that, Lenna sat on a bed and immediately fell asleep.

*   *   *

When Lenna awoke, she found that she was alone in the room. There was a note on the floor next to her bed.

> "Lenna,
>   Let's see that power of yours. Find your way out.
>
>   ~Divy"

Lenna stared at the paper. She looked around the room at the identical walls. There was no obvious exit. She looked at the paper again, hoping to find something which she hadn't seen before. Luckily, she found what she needed on the opposite side.

"Divy likes playing tricks on people. I'm sorry, it's stupid. I can't give you the answer though, or he'll get mad. Here's a hint: Try getting in touch with the walls.

Good luck,
Mira"

Lenna went to one of the walls. "Get in touch with the walls?" she asked. "That makes no sense!" She thought for a moment, and then focused on the word "touch". She lifted her hand and knocked. A soft tapping sound came from it. She went to another wall and heard the same sound. Then, she went to the third wall and heard a louder tap. She extended her hands, moved one upwards and one downwards, and the wall slid out of the way, revealing her four new friends waiting for her.

"Took you long enough," Divy said. "We're ready when you are." The four from Ixie had a large sack next to each of them.

"How about giving her something to eat on the way?" Mira asked Divy impatiently. She handed Lenna a small piece of bread with meat inside of it. Lenna ate the peculiar yet delicious food as they walked out of the room. "Divy made that."

When they emerged, Lenna found that they weren't at the pond, but came walking right out of the ground. This was Kita's entrance.

The group walked to the beach and found Lenna's slightly damaged ship. They each climbed aboard.

"This'll be easy," Mira said, standing under the ship's sail and sending small gusts of wind into it, making it ripple. Divy stood on one side and began to move the water under the ship, picking it up and letting it drift.

"Lenna, help me out," he said. Lenna stood on the other side of the ship and began to help move the water. Soon the ship was rapidly moving out to sea, and Lenna smiled as she prepared to return home.

Chapter 2:
Paro

A slightly damaged boat floated down a river inside of a thick forest. Dimi was sitting on the bow, looking around curiously. He'd been sailing for about nine weeks and was anxious to explore this new place. The boy had a strong body, tan skin, and long, wavy brown hair which touched right below his ears. Inside of his pocket was his knife which could change into any weapon he chose. A single blue gem was embedded in the blade.

The boat came to the end of the river and touched the land next to it. Dimi jumped out and began to walk through the forest. The entire island was covered in trees and he had yet to see a single person. He guessed that the warrior he'd find here would be the tree. As he walked through the forest, he kept his eyes open and attentive, but saw no tree with only two branches. Alert for the other possibilities as well, he took note of every detail around him. He saw many animals, but no snakes, nor a boy with wings.

"It's definitely the tree . . ." Dimi thought, focusing on his surroundings. He frowned. He didn't want to check every single tree in the whole forest.

Dimi walked for hours. He found nothing that would be of any help to him, and slowly the sun set without him realizing. He was lost without light, yet he continued to move. As he walked with his hands held out in front of him, feeling for trees, he tried to think about what he would say to the warriors once he found them. Before he could decide on anything though, he was distracted by something in the distance. Behind the trees he saw a dim glow. He ran towards it, careful not to trip over any roots, and stepped into a small clearing. There were six small huts built around a massive bon fire. A group of people turned and saw him, and he stepped forward in an attempt to speak to them. Their reaction was fearful.

"Get inside," someone whispered, but not to him. A group of women and children ran into the huts, leaving six men and three boys standing opposite Dimi, spears in hand. "Who are you?" one of the men asked.

"I'm Dimi. I come from Sio," Dimi answered.

"Sio?" asked one of the boys. "Where's that?" He was addressing one of the men.

"It's another island," Dimi answered.

"There are no other islands in this world except ours," said a large man. "You're lying to us. You are our enemy." The man stepped forward and picked up a spear from the ground.

"Please, I don't want to fight! Look, I'll give up my weapon!" Dimi said, pulling his knife from his pocket.

"He has weapons!" shouted one of the boys. "Kill him!" Dimi pocketed his knife and sprinted out of the area. The men pursued him, running quickly through the forest which they knew much better in the dark than he did. As he ran, his shoulders scraped the sides of the trees and his ankles were pulled on by the plants beneath him. Heavy rocks began to hit him on his head and back. Overhead, the three boys were jumping from branch to branch, pelting him. Dimi tried to move fast, but his efforts were worthless. The men were quicker than he was, and they were soon right behind him.

Dimi's face hit the ground. He had tripped over a root, and the men were now standing over him. One of the boys in the branches lit a small torch which he held over the scene, revealing the large man standing directly at Dimi's feet. The man raised his spear directly over Dimi's head and thrust it down at his face.

The spear never came in contact with Dimi's head, though. A loud hiss stretched through the air, and the spear stopped directly above Dimi's nose. Something moved alongside his arm, but the boy didn't dare avert his eyes from the weapon being held over him.

"Leave here, Luc," said the man. "He's our problem to deal with." The hiss came again, this time louder. Dimi looked over and saw a snake looking up at the men. It was as green as the leaves on the trees, and it had two fangs coming out from the sides of its mouth. Dimi's eyes lit up with excitement. "I said leave!" the man shouted at the snake. It did not leave, though. Instead, it lifted itself up so it was eye level with the man. It opened its mouth, showing its teeth, and gave an authoritative hiss, almost like a growl. The man put his spear at his side, turned, and led the others away. Then the snake turned to Dimi.

"Thank you," Dimi said, sitting up. However, the snake hissed angrily at him, and he fell back down. It slithered over to his feet and stopped. Then, it began to grow. It lost its shape and took on the figure of a human. It grew legs, arms, and a human face. It lost its tail and scales and changed into a pale boy of Dimi's age. He was tall and wore a green tunic with green pants which matched the color of the snake. "How did you do that?" Dimi asked.

"It's my power, and the fact that you don't know that means that you're not from our island. Who are you?" the boy asked seriously.

"My name's Dimi. I come from Sio."

"Sio?"

"It's another island. There are four other islands. You've had no contact with them?"

"I had no idea there are any other islands, and I hardly believe I should trust you."

"Please, listen. I'm a warrior just like you! In fact, I've been looking for you specifically. If you take me to the other warriors here, I'll explain everything."

"The other warriors? Why do you call them warriors? We are protectors!" the boy said proudly.

"Is there a difference?" Dimi reasoned. The boy was silent. Then he lifted his tunic to show a belt around his waist. He took it off and rubbed something on it.

"I'm coming back, and we might have a problem. Be on your guard," he said to the belt. Then he put it back around his waist.

"Communication gems!" Dimi stated.

"How do you know about them?" the boy asked.

"I have them too!" Dimi said, pulling out his knife and showing the blue gem embedded in the blade. Again, the boy was silent.

"I don't believe you. I don't trust you. You're lucky to be alive right now, and you're lucky that my friends will want to meet you. Let's go," he said, and he quickly shrunk back into his snake form and began to slither off. Dimi followed him. They traveled for a few minutes before Dimi saw another clearing with a fire and three huts. The fire wasn't as bright here as in the other clearing, but he was able to make out two bodies standing next to it.

"What is it?" asked a girl's voice. The snake changed back into the boy.

"This boy says that he comes from Sio, another island. He says that he has protectors on his island, and he's one of them. He's proved this by showing his communication gem, but I still don't think we should trust him," the boy said, shoving Dimi forward.

"If he's a protector, then why shouldn't we trust him?" asked a boy's voice.

"He could be here to take over our side of the island!" Luc said.

"No! That's not why I'm here!" Dimi said defensively.

"Quiet!"

"Let him talk!" the girl said. She stood up and pushed the snake-boy aside. "Luc can be extremely hostile. Give him time to get used to you, and forgive him, please," she whispered to Dimi. "Luc, you shouldn't be worried about which side controls which. It's our job to stay neutral through this and avoid conflict."

"It's also our job to prevent conflict," Luc responded. He turned to Dimi. "Talk."

"I'm here to ask for your help," he said to the group. "All of you. Sio is under the control of an evil man, and my friends and I can't take him down alone. We tried once and failed, so four of us set out to find the warriors from the four other islands in the world. I was sent here. At least I think I was. This *is* Paro, isn't it?"

"It is," said the girl. "Continue."

"Each of us is supposed to bring the warriors from the other islands back to Sio to help us, so I'm asking you all to please come back with me."

"What if something happens here while we're gone?" asked the girl.

"Hopefully you won't be gone for too long, but if something happens, we'll gladly come to help you resolve it," Dimi answered. "Please, we need your help."

"What's your power?" asked the third member of the group. It was the boy.

"I have this knife," Dimi answered, showing it to them. "It can change into any weapon that I want." The knife began to glow blue, and then grew into a large sword. "See?" It shrunk back into its normal form again.

The girl walked over to a large pile of logs a few feet from the fire. She picked up a few and threw them onto the flames, making the light much brighter. Dimi could see everyone clearly now. "I'm Vesa," she said. "I transform into a fish." Vesa had black hair which was held up in two ponytails. She wore a purple tunic and skirt. Two hooked knives were attached to her waist. Around her ankle was a bracelet, and Dimi could see her gems shining. She looked to be fifteen years old, like he and Luc.

"Feo," said the second boy. He had spiked blonde hair and wore a silver tunic and pants. A loose necklace hung around his neck and displayed his gems. He was tall and appeared fifteen years old as well. "I change into a bird."

"Well it's nice to meet you all," Dimi said. "So what do you think? Will you come back to Sio with me?" There was silence. The three from Paro stared at each other, as if attempting to have a silent conversation. Vesa spoke.

"No," she said, "we can't. You're here at at a horrible time. You've come right in the middle of a three-sided civil war, and it's our jobs as protectors to . . . well, protect, so we have to stay here and keep the people of Paro safe from themselves. This island is bigger than it seems, and the tribes here obviously don't get along. That's where we come in. If we leave here, the entire island will destroy itself."

"So how about one of you stays here?" Dimi suggested. "The other two can come back to Sio with me."

"Don't you understand our powers?" Luc heatedly asked. "A bird, a snake, and a fish. We keep the island at peace from the air, the land, and the sea. Without all three of us, the protectors are

16

incomplete. What happens then when the animal that's needed isn't here?"

"Why can't the people here live at peace?" Dimi asked. "Let's solve their problems and then leave."

"If it was that simple we wouldn't be in this mess," Luc answered. "That's why we can't leave. And frankly, you shouldn't have left Sio. It's *your* home, *you* protect it." Dimi stepped forward, angered at this comment.

"My friends and I risked our lives to help the people of our island, and we failed. I can *admit* that we failed. That's why I'm here. Forgive me for not having someone like you there to fix everything, make everyone happy, and have time to tie our shoes as well."

"Shoes?" Feo asked. Dimi stared at him, unable to comprehend the question. He then looked down and acknowledged Feo's bare feet. Vesa and Luc's feet were the same, and for some reason, Vesa was grinning.

"These," Dimi answered, moving his foot and showing his sandals. Feo nodded.

"They look uncomfortable."

"Let's talk more about this in the morning," Vesa said. "Dimi, you can sleep in Luc's hut." She motioned to one of three huts standing behind them.

"Then where will I sleep?!" Luc protested loudly.

"Quiet," Vesa whispered. "You can stay in mine." They smiled at each other. Dimi gave Feo a look as if asking if they were serious, and Feo nodded. They all separated to their respective quarters, Luc a little too eager to retire for the night.

*   *   *

Dimi laid awake in Luc's bed, unable to sleep in a place where he knew he was not welcome. He thought about his friends back on Sio. He missed them all, especially Ellia. He thought of her and tried to imagine her being there with him. He was comforted, but right as he was about to drift into sleep he heard someone approaching his room.

"Can I come in?" sounded a whisper. It was Feo.

"Sure," Dimi answered, sitting up. Feo stepped into the room and held up a large book to Dimi.

"There's one way that we could come with you," he said. Feo opened the book to the first page. He read the words aloud to Dimi.

"'The five from the forest will guard the peace, and the island will prosper and grow. Soaring from the skies, creeping through the ground, splashing from the ocean, flittering through the breeze, and stomping along the dirt, these five will appear and keep Paro in harmony.' That's what it says."

"I don't understand," Dimi said.

"It says that there are supposed to be five of us, and yet we only have three. If we could find the other two, maybe we could figure out a way that some of us could stay here and some of us could go with you."

"But Vesa said that the island is big. I don't have that much time to stay and search with you. I need to get home."

"Then go," Feo said. "Take Vesa and Luc with you and leave me here. I'll find the other two and then let you know what's going to happen."

"No, I can't do that. Luc and Vesa won't go, and I can't leave you here by yourself."

"Yes you can, and they won't have a choice. We're going to sneak them onto your boat and away from here."

"No! Do you hear yourself? This is crazy talk!"

"This is sensible talk. I don't care what Luc says, you aren't leaving here without at least one of us. I can handle it here by myself."

"Then you and Luc stay here at least. I'll bring Vesa. She might go."

"Yeah so she can flop around on dry land and do absolutely nothing? Good plan." There was silence. "Look, Luc was right about how our group completes itself: one in the air, one on the land, and one in the sea. However, the one in the air can fly low to the group and along the water as well. Besides, the two of them won't leave unless the other leaves as well." There was silence again as Feo stared at Dimi.

"How do we get them onto the boat?" he finally asked.

"Good," Feo said. "Now, that's the tricky part. We only have a small amount of time to move them, and that time is being wasted as we speak. Vesa and Luc have . . . exhausted themselves, if you know what I mean, and so we have to move them while they're sleeping deeply. Let's go!" Feo dashed out of the room, leaving a wide-eyed Dimi behind him. Dimi walked out and into Vesa's hut where he found Feo holding a large bag.

"Here," he said, handing Dimi the bag. "Fill it with Vesa's clothes." Dimi stared at the bag, and then looked at Vesa and Luc, who were sleeping in each others arms.

"Things like that are frowned upon on Sio," Dimi whispered.

"Things like that are frowned upon here too, but that doesn't stop them. Fill that bag! Don't forget her knives; she'll kill you if she doesn't have them. Where's your boat?"

"She'll kill me anyway! And I have no idea!" Dimi whispered. "It's in some river."

"Oh, I know that river!" Feo said. Dimi stared at him, astonished. "There's only one on this side of the island. I'll bring them there and then come back to get you. Pack clothes from Luc's room when you're finished in here."

"How are you going to get them there?" Dimi whispered, stuffing the bag with identical purple tunics. He turned and looked at Feo, who had already changed into a large, majestic, silver bird. Feo flapped his wings, hovering in the air, and grabbed the edge of Vesa's mattress with his talons. He slowly began to drag the mattress out of the hut and into the forest. "You'll hit bumps!" Dimi whispered loudly, following Feo out, but the bird had already disappeared into the trees.

After raiding Vesa's drawers and packing her clothes, Dimi walked back into Luc's hut and filled up the bag with his identical green tunics and pants. Once finished, he stepped out and waited for Feo, who returned minutes later.

"I need your help," Feo said after changing back into a human. "I didn't really think about the part when we move them from the land onto the boat."

"You're telling me that you moved them all the way to the river without them waking up?" Dimi asked, shocked.

"Yes, easily," Feo casually said. "My bird form isn't a normal one. But I need to get them up onto the boat. Let's go, come on!" He jumped into the air, his body bursting into the form of a bird, and shot through the trees. Dimi, grabbing the bag, sprinted along the same path as Feo, but he quickly lost track of his guide. He could hardly see his hand in front of his face. It wasn't long before he walked directly into a tall tree, causing various seeds to fall onto his head.

As Dimi stood up, he felt something crawling on his neck. He slapped the spot that was tickling him. Something else was crawling along his forearm. He slapped that spot too, feeling the successful crush of a bug under his hand. Two more bugs crawled up his leg. He crushed them as well. Soon Dimi felt an entire swarm of insects crawling over his body. He whimpered slightly and then ran as fast as he could from the spot, rubbing every inch of his body to make sure that they weren't still on him.

Just as he was beginning to feel comfortable again, he tripped and landed in a large pile of mud. Wiping his face, he felt for what he had tripped over. It felt like a rough, leathery body. Something grunted. Dimi struggled to stand and then continued to run, afraid of what had made the noise. Somewhere behind him, a tree toppled over.

"You woke up a rhybuck!" someone shouted. Feo was running next to him.

"When did you get here?!" Dimi shouted back.

"I know this island better than anyone else; it was easy to find you. Come this way, quick, we're being chased."

"By what?!" Dimi ran after him.

"The rhybuck! Haven't you been listening?"

"What's a rhybuck?"

"It'll kill you with one stab of the horn on its nose! Two stabs from the horn on its tail! This way." Feo made a hard left and stopped short. They had arrived at the river and were standing right next to the still sleeping Vesa and Luc. "Quick, they're going to wake up soon," Feo whispered. He changed into the bird and lifted the foot of the bed. Dimi could barely lift the head, but they were able to move the sleeping couple onto the boat without waking them. Right as they finished, Vesa rolled over, moaning angrily, but then fell back asleep.

"How are they sleeping through all of this?" Dimi whispered. Another tree fell somewhere in the forest.

"With animals like rhybucks roaming freely, we learn to sleep through the disturbances," Feo answered. "Now leave! I'll see you soon. Good luck!" Dimi stepped onto the boat and looked at Feo, who pushed it away from the land and into the water. The boat slowly drifted down the river and out into the ocean.

As Paro disappeared into the distance, Dimi sat down and wondered if what he had just done was wrong.

"I think I just kidnapped people," he thought to himself as he fell asleep. His comfort didn't last long, however. A few hours later, the sun began to rise.

Before he had time to come to his senses, he was being lifted by his collar high into the air. A hooked knife was wrapping lightly around his throat. "Oh, you better have a good explanation for this." Dimi's eyes snapped open, revealing Vesa, one hand holding his collar, the other holding the knife. A shirtless Luc was frantically putting pants on.

Chapter 3: Helite

Waves crashed upon the shore of a giant island. As they rolled away, Ruller's body was left sprawled on the sand. The boy lied face down, trying to gain the strength to breathe. He gasped for air and rolled over, only to be hit by another wave coming onto the shore. He crawled away from the shoreline, tears streaming from his eyes, and looked out at the water. He could just make out the broken remains of his boat floating on the waves, returning to the sea. If this island wasn't Helite, he'd be in trouble.

Ruller had been at sea a little less than eight weeks and sailed into the great storm, completely destroying his boat and sending him hurdling overboard. To make matters worse, his book of spells was gone as well.

Just before the storm hit a spell appeared on one of the blank pages of his book, giving him the power to create an energy shield around him. With the book still open on the deck of the boat, the rocking of the waves moved it overboard and down to the bottom of the ocean. Before Ruller could fuss over this loss, though, he was caught in the storm. If that new spell hadn't appeared, he would've drowned.

He sat up and stared at the sea. His book, his most valuable possession, was gone. He held out a hand toward the ocean. *"Coget book!"* His summoning spell failed, and he began to panic. *"Coget book!"* Again, nothing appeared. His eyes were filling with tears. "Please . . ." he whispered hopelessly. At this word, violet light began to shine through the sand in front of him. A new spell book identical to the one he had lost appeared at his feet. He let his tears run down his face as he picked it up and held on to it like it was his lost child. He began to shuffle through the pages. They were exactly like his old book, with his spells in the front and various blank pages in the back. To his surprise, though, there was a new spell on one of the front pages.

"Fire Spell:
  'Plumis'"

Ruller opened his hand and pointed it towards the sea once more. *"Plumis!"* A jet of flames shot out from the palm of his hand, slowly pushing him down against the sand. Uncomfortable, he whined and tried to adjust the strength of the flames. He closed his hand slightly, and the flames became smaller. Soon he had a small glow hovering over his wiggling fingers. With his newfound power, he stood up and turned to look at the island, only to realize that he was facing a giant hill. He began to climb, and as he reached the top, a beautiful, radiant, and perfect landscape was revealed to him.

A large castle was set in the far distance. It had many tall towers and was surrounded by a small town. There were patches of trees dispersed throughout the land, as well as many rolling plains. Ruller couldn't see the other side of the island past the plains.

He began to walk towards the castle. The first place he wanted to look was in the town, but something stopped him in his tracks. Off in the distance, something spiraled into the air. It was farther than the castle, and looked almost like a snake, its body being long and slender, only it had a head in the shape of a lightning bolt, the bottom of which merged into its neck. There were no legs or arms, but it had two large, feathered wings coming out of its back. The detail which attracted Ruller's attention the most, though, was a thin beam shooting out of the top of the creature's head. The creature seemed to be enraged, and he wanted to help it.

"Anla fro Helite portran ... over there!" he shouted. Nothing happened. *"Anla fro Helite portran Helite castle?"* This time the boy disappeared and reappeared miles away directly outside of the castle. He turned to where he thought he saw the flying snake and ran out of the town and in that direction. He could see more of the island from over here. There were mountains to

his left and a vast forest directly in front of him. He ran through the trees.

Ruller ran for as long as he could, and then stopped to catch his breath. He stepped softly on the ground, trying to make as little noise as possible in order to avoid scaring the creature away should it be lurking nearby. The forest didn't seem to have an edge. In fact, Ruller was sure that he was now lost. He had been walking for a while, and everything had started to look the same. He suddenly stumbled over something. He turned around, but there was nothing there. He turned back around and walked directly into a tree. He could have sworn it wasn't there before. Something was odd about this forest. There was a sound behind him, but he turned to see nothing but a line of trees. He didn't think there were that many trees the last time he looked. He turned back around and found another line of trees in front of him. He was completely boxed in, and the only thing to do was squeeze between two of them. He did this with great difficulty and popped out into a clearing. There was a large nest in the middle made of leaves and twigs, and Ruller walked over and sat down upon it.

A shriek came from somewhere nearby and the creature erupted out of the trees again. It seemed to be only a few acres away from him, and he could see more details of it. Its body was yellow on top which merged into a light blue bottom. The most shocking part of the creature, however, was the boy riding on top of its back. The boy looked to be about sixteen years old, and he was focused as the creature flew away quickly.

"Come back!" Ruller called. "*Rili!*" he shouted, opening his hand and thrusting it into the air. He flew up and hovered above the trees. He could see the creature flying off into an area near the water. Before he could take note of where, his spell wore off and he plummeted back through the trees. "*RILI!*" he screamed, and he hovered for a moment, and then fell the rest of the way down, landing in the nest.

As he came to his senses he noticed that something was different about the clearing. A small tree now stood in the middle. It had two branches coming out from the top of it. Ruller thought that the tree looked oddly familiar. He stood up and stepped towards it, and then remembered that it was exactly like the tree he had walked into before. He looked at it closely. It really was *exactly* like the tree he had walked into. That was the first odd thing about it. The second was that the tree seemed to be looking back at him. The lines in its bark bent like a face. He could see two eyes, a nose, and a mouth. In fact, the tree looked like a person standing with its arms in the air.

"Boo!" A face extended out of the bark. Ruller screamed and fell backwards.

"What are you?!" he shouted.

"Iu ec?" the tree asked. Its branches fell to its sides and took the form of arms and hands. Its narrow trunk curved into a girl's body, and its leaves extended into short brown hair with two locks coming over a thin headband and extending over the girl's face. Ruller thought that she looked to be about sixteen years old. She had tan skin and was average height. "U es iu?" she asked him.

"Huh?" he asked. The girl stepped forward and looked him in the eye. Then, her face changed to look exactly like his. She shrunk down to his size, her hair shortened to his hair's length, and she was even wearing the same clothes as him. Before he could react, she began to speak to him.

"Your name is Ruller. You're nine years old and come from Sio. You are the youngest member of the Circle Stone Group, specializing in magic spells which are shown to you by the book which you always carry by your side. Your best friend is a girl named Shenny, put first only because you have known her longer than these girls Vicky and Ursa." She changed back into her normal form. "My name is Maura. By looking you in the eye and changing into you, I've learned your language and everything about you. By changing back I've forgotten what I knew about you, but kept the language in order to communicate better. Don't worry, I won't invade your privacy and change into you again. Now, why do you want that dragon?"

Ruller stared at her. "Maura? You become people?"

"I'm a shapeshifter," she answered, "I become anything I want. If I look someone directly in the eye, I can become them, adopting all of their memories and habits. I didn't want to stay like you for long because I didn't want to be rude and invade your mind like that. Now, about that dragon you were chasing."

"I just wanted to see why it was angry," he answered innocently. Maura stared at him.

"Why have people from Sio come here?" she finally asked.

"Are you a warrior?" Ruller asked.

"Yes. What do you want with me?"

"My friends and I need your help to take Sio back from an evil man named Gabent. He took over Sio and destroyed everything, and now we're in hiding. Four of us left to the four different islands of the world to find the other warriors to help us, and I was sent here. Will you help me?"

Maura was silent. "If you want us all, it'll take some effort. Kit will be easy to convince, but Maia is a challenge. Come back to our base and meet Kit. Use your teleporting spell to take us there." Ruller's eyes widened. "Okay, fine, I took note of your spells, too. I wanted to make sure that you weren't a threat."

Ruller took her hand. "*Anla fro Helite portran Helite warriors' base!*" The two of them disappeared and reappeared in a small, undecorated room with a fire blazing in the middle. A thirteen year old boy sat on the ground, staring at them. He had long brown hair which flowed below his shirt collar, a bony body, and a fairly large head.

"Maura?" he asked. "Ec e iu?"

"Ruller e on nos," she said. "Eda eron ed noseb al e unnel snad e nosa as. Suv sed eu?"

"Uo sup, suon ed oseb a lis," the boy answered.

"Ruller, this is Kit. He can change objects into other objects as long as he has a piece of the object he's changing it into. Get it?" Ruller nodded. "He said that he'd help you, so you have two of us on your side. Like I said before, Maia will be a challenge. She's stubborn, pompous, and ungrateful, and she won't hesitate to throw you out of her sight. She's also the weakest of the three of us, which makes her bitter. There's only one way to get to her, and that's with Duner's help."

"Why is she going to be such a challenge, though? And who's Duner?" Ruller asked.

"I'm sure you noticed the castle when you first arrived here. How could you miss it? She lives there. She's our princess."

"The princess is a warrior?!" Ruller exclaimed.

"Well is there a rule saying that it can only be unimportant people?" Maura asked. "Now before we waste anymore time, I'll go call Duner. We only have a little daylight left, and this all has to happen at night." Maura left the room. Ruller smiled at Kit, and he returned the smile. The rest of the time was spent in awkward silence. Finally, Maura returned. "He'll be here in a few minutes. Duner isn't a warrior, but he's the only person who knows about us. He's my best friend. We've been through a lot together."

"I know what you mean," Ruller smiled. "Back on Sio, there are actually two groups of warriors, not one. There are the original warriors, called the Circle Stone Group, and there are four others. They helped us in our first fight against Gabent, and when they met Sio, he made them official warriors, even though he couldn't give them any powers. Shenny is one of the new warriors. It's nice to have friends."

"You have a name for your group?!" Maura asked. "I'm jealous! I want a special name for our group!" Ruller was astounded by her sudden change to a more casual attitude.

"Didn't Helite give you one?" he asked.

"We've never met Helite. We know that she exists, but we've never seen her."

"Well then I'll give you a name. Let me meet Maia first so I can see what her powers are. Unless you want to tell me now," Ruller said, hopefully.

"It's not my place," Maura answered, smiling. "Besides, if you went in there knowing what her powers were, she'd go on a rant about how we were making fun of her and how the whole world is against her. Lies! Just because she doesn't get along with us doesn't mean that we make fun of her!"

"Okay, calm down," Ruller said, sensing anger.

"Maura!" Kit whined.

"Uo?" she asked, turning to him.

"Elrap su eu ec ed roas eu ej!" he whined.

"What's he saying?" Ruller asked.

"He wants to know what we're talking about . . . Hmm . . . Oh, I know! When I tell you, I want you to just start talking. Say anything you want." Ruller nodded. "Kit, erl ne stom ses reac. Okay Ruller, speak." Ruller began to babble. Kit stood up and pointed at Ruller's mouth. Light purple rings began to expand out of his finger and float towards Ruller's mouth. Confused, the boy continued to speak. Then, he choked and began to gasp for breath. A book appeared out of the air right in front of him, and it was sucking all of the air out of him. Finally, the book shut and Ruller collapsed.

"What was that?!" he asked hoarsely.

"I'm sorry!" Maura said. "He needed something to make a book that would translate our two languages, and since we have no paper here, I decided to use your language. That's why I had you speak. I'm sorry!"

"You couldn't have used a piece of paper from my book?"

"Kit still wouldn't have known what to use to make the language." This detail confused Ruller, so he didn't say anything and stayed on the floor for a moment, catching his breath. Kit walked over and picked up the book. He flipped through the pages.

"I . . . am . . . sorry," he said, smiling.

"Is sus ej!" said a voice. A boy with long brown hair had appeared in the doorway of the room. He looked oddly familiar. Maura ran over to him and hugged him. Then she began to babble to him in Helitian. His face drained and he seemed worried. He answered her back, and then took a large staff out of a pouch attached to his belt. It was dark blue and had a small, square hole in the top, resembling a lantern. On top of this were three spikes. Maura seemed to be pleading with Duner, and then she turned to Ruller.

"I can't come with you to the castle. Duner is going to do something to my powers that is going to make me too weak to even walk. Trust Duner and Kit, they'll be going with you. When you get into the castle, don't take no for an answer. Keep persisting and fight with her if you have to. Good luck." She turned her back on Ruller and held out her hands. Something red was glowing in them, and it looked like Duner was touching the staff to it. The glow became brighter and then dimmed. Maura fainted into Duner's arms. He laid her on the ground and then motioned for Ruller and Kit to follow him out of the room. Kit followed, but Ruller hesitated, unsure if he should check on Maura or not. She was motionless on the floor and her eyes were shut. However, he obeyed her orders and did as Duner had told him.

When they went outside, Ruller found that they were in the middle of a plain, and sitting right in front of him was the dragon which he had seen earlier that day. Now he understood why Duner looked familiar to him. The dragon bent its head down and stared Ruller in the eye. Then it looked at Duner. The boy nodded, and the dragon bent its head low to the ground. Duner patted it. "Esofos," he said. Then he jumped onto Esofos's back. Kit followed and then helped Ruller up. They took off.

As they flew, the sun quickly set and stars dotted the sky. Soon they arrived at the castle. Esofos wove between the towers and began circling one while climbing upwards. Ruller would have fallen off if it wasn't for Kit grabbing onto his shirt to keep him steady. They flew higher and were soon above all the other towers. Finally, they reached the top. Windows lined an area right below the tower's spire, and Esofos flew alongside the windows so that they could see inside.

They looked into what seemed to be a throne room. There was a large, circular platform in the room, and on it was an extremely decorated throne. Sitting on the throne was an eighteen year old girl. She had bright red hair, almost pink, which was pulled back into two very long ponytails behind her head. The ponytails reached down below her waist. She wore a headband across her forehead just like Maura did. In fact, it looked almost exactly like Maura's. The only difference between the two was their colors. The girl's was pink and Maura's was crimson. The girl also wore a deep purple dress with a pink sash around her extremely small waist.

"That . . . is Maia," Kit said, flipping through his book. "We . . . will . . . go . . . in . . . there . . . while Duner . . . waits . . . out . . . here."

"Okay," Ruller said. "How do we get in?" Kit stared at him, puzzled. He forgot that Kit and Duner couldn't understand him.

He took Kit's book and looked up what he wanted to say. "Son norne nemoc?"

"Cec emoc," Duner answered. Esofos reeled back and flew directly into the window. He flew into the room and Duner pushed Ruller and Kit off. Then they flew out, leaving the two boys lying on the ground. Maia was screaming.

"Quiet!" Ruller shouted, worried that someone might hear her.

"Oh, a Sioite," she said. She raised an eyebrow at him and made an uptight face

"How do you know my language?" Ruller asked. Maia took off her headband.

"See this? It means I'm a princess, and that means that I'm taught about the entire world. Now what do you want before I call my guards on you."

"We just want to talk to you," Ruller said calmly. "I need your help. You're a warrior, and that means that I need you to come back to Sio with me to help me and my friends fight off an evil man named Gabent."

"No."

"But you have to!" Ruller persisted.

"No."

"Why not?"

"Why should I? It's not my problem."

"But it could be your problem. Who knows what he'll do now that he has Sio. He might come here next."

"If that's the case, then I'll fight him off."

"By yourself? There are eleven warriors on Sio and we couldn't beat him. What makes you so sure that you can?"

"My powers give me the advantage. I have two." Maia stood up from her throne and spun around. She vanished into thin air. Then she reappeared in the same spot. "That's the first. I can also open portals between two places. Watch." The princess closed her eyes and took a deep breath. Then she opened them again and concentrated on a spot right in front of her. She extended her arms and clenched her fingers around something in the air. She moved her arms apart, and something green and swirling appeared in front of her. It seemed that she had torn a hole in the air in front of her. She stepped into it and it closed. Ruller felt a hand on his shoulder. "Neat, huh?" She ran one of her nails across his throat. "You'd be dead right now."

"How did you get behind me?!" he asked, shocked.

"How do you think?" Maia answered. She began to walk back to her chair. "Now give me one reason why I shouldn't have you thrown out of here."

"Because I need your help! My friends need your help! Everyone on Sio needs your help! Without you, the Helite warriors are incomplete."

"Yes, I see you've already gotten the other two on your side. Hi, Kit," Maia said, acknowledging the boy for the first time.

"Hi," Kit answered back.

"Oh! You've taught him words! I'm surprised that he's capable of remembering them."

"He has a book," Ruller said, annoyed, "and if you were as ambitious as he is, we could be gone by now."

"Don't compare me to him! I'm better than him—better than both of them!" Maia shrieked.

"That's not true!" Ruller shouted. "You three are a team and you should act as equals!" At that, the room fell silent except for Kit flipping through his book in order to keep up with the conversation. Maia stepped down from her platform and walked over to Kit. She knocked the book out of his hands and onto the floor.

"They're weak, and I'm better than them," she said.

"Weak?!" Ruller shouted, but before he could say anything else, Kit had grabbed Maia's shoulders and spun her so she faced him. He pointed directly at her. Purple rings shot out of his finger and surrounded Maia's clothing. Almost instantly the fabrics of her dress changed into fur covered lizards. The girl was screaming at the top of her lungs.

"GET THEM OFF OF ME! THEY'RE DISGUSTING! GET THEM OFF!" she screamed.

"What are they?" Ruller asked, not moving from his spot.

"Hizards!" Maia said frantically. "My clothes are made from their fur. Now get them off!"

"No, I don't think I will," Ruller said. "I think I'm too weak. You're so strong, you get them off." Maia spun around. She disappeared, but the hizards didn't. They were still holding onto her invisible body. She reappeared.

"It's not working!"

"Why do your clothes disappear when you become invisible, but the hizards don't?"

"I don't know! My clothes always have!"

"Will you come back to Sio with me?" The girl stopped moving.

"No. SEGAR! EDA!" she screamed.

"DUNER!" Kit shouted. He frantically flipped through his book. "Get . . . her . . . out!" he said to Ruller. He pointed at the hizards. The purple rings shot at them and they changed into hizard fur ropes.

"*Rili!*" Ruller shouted. Maia began to float into the air. She screamed. At that moment, the guards came bursting through the door.

"Eserp Maia!" they shouted.

"*Rili!*" Ruller and Kit began to float into the air as well. As if planned, Duner and Esofos flew through the window and scooped the three of them up. They flew away.

"Bring me back! Let me go!" Maia screamed as they soared through the sky.

"No, you're coming back to the base with us and you're going to talk to Maura," Ruller said.

"No! She's the last person I want to speak to! I'm not going to be told what to do by a little kid!"

"Too bad!" Ruller said harshly. "You're tied up!"

They soon arrived back in the plain. They stepped inside the base while Esofos curled up to take a nap in the grass. When they entered, they found Maura sitting up, waiting for them.

"How did it go?" she asked weakly.

"How do you think?" Maia answered before Ruller could. Ruller noticed Kit step forward and lift his finger at Maia's harsh tone, but he stopped him. Instead, Kit pointed at the ropes. The rings shot out of his finger and Maia's clothes returned to normal.

"Aren't you going to say thank you?" Ruller asked her.

"No," she answered.

"That's it! What is your problem?!" Ruller shouted.

"Don't shout at me!" Maia screamed. "I don't want to be here, I don't want these powers, and I don't want anything to do with any of you! Let me leave and go back to my castle!" The girl turned and proceeded to stomp out of the room.

"*Coget Maia!*" Ruller screamed. The girl was pulled back and into Ruller's outstretched hand. The boy, though small, threw her to the ground and stood over her. Sparks were erupting from his fingers. "You're lazy! You're lazy and spoiled and I'm tired of your attitude! Face it, you're weak! What're you going to do if I attack you, huh? Turn invisible and then pick up a stick to hit me with it? Guess what? I can still see the stick and it won't do much to hurt me! See this book? There are spells in this book that could tear you apart, invisible or not, and it is so easy for me to say the words to them. Oh, and opening a portal during battle isn't that great of an idea either. You leave the battle and whatever you're fighting for perishes. It's time you accept that you have powers and learn how to use them, like it or not." The room was silent. Suddenly Ruller turned and faced Maura. "And don't think that you're not at fault either! You and Kit should be helping Maia instead of ignoring her, because that's not going to solve anything!" The room fell silent again. Maura stepped forward.

"When are we leaving?" she asked timidly. It was obvious that the girl was scared to make Ruller angrier than he already was.

"Right now. You're bringing what you have with you and we're leaving," the boy answered.

"But I—," Maia started.

"Quiet!" Ruller shouted at her. Maura was speaking rapidly to Kit and Duner, letting them know what was going on. Then she turned to Maia.

"Your brother can rule while you're gone. Duner will tell him to. Ruller, can we teleport out of here?" Maura asked.

"No," he answered. "We're not teleporting anywhere. Maia will open a portal and bring us there. It's time she started to work." Maia, however, was not done arguing. She sat on the floor and crossed her arms, raising an eyebrow at Ruller. His body began to shake as his angry emotions got the best of him. *"Plumis,"* he said, pulling his hands into tight fists. Fire swirled around his wrists and circled his hands. He stepped towards Maia and held his fist in front of her face. "Don't make me release this." Maia slowly stood up and brought her hands together. She separated them and the swirling green hole appeared in front of her. Duner stepped back and waved good bye. "Isn't he coming?" he asked Maura.

"He's not a warrior, remember? Besides, he's needed here on Helite." Maura stepped into the portal and disappeared. Kit quickly followed her. Maia stood next to the portal with her hand on its edge, keeping it open. Ruller jumped in and Maia quickly followed. The portal closed.

Chapter 4: Cumber

The sky was bright and sunny. Vicky jumped down onto a beach from her boat. She had been at sea for five weeks and was happy to be back on land.

Vicky stood in the sand. She looked around at the island before her. It was quite barren. The sand beneath her stretched up the land a little before hitting a light tan rock. The entire area was made up of this rock, and a single giant, steep, and cylindrical mountain loomed over the area. The mountain was about fifteen miles away from where the girl sat, and a strip of small rock hills extended out from its sides and stretched to the edges of the island.

She looked down at the gloves on her hands. Six small, green gems dotted them, and Vicky rubbed one of them. She looked at it closely and saw Ursa's face.

"Ursa!" she whispered. She watched her sister glance at her, and then walk to another area.

"Vicky, we're not supposed to be talking! You know that!" Ursa said.

"I know, but I wanted to tell you that I think I've found Cumber!"

"That's great!" Ursa said. She smiled widely at her sister.

"How is everyone there?" Vicky asked.

"They've been better. Things haven't been the same since what happened with Chaily, but they're all fine. I really shouldn't be talking, though. They'll hear me. It was great seeing you!"

"I miss you! I'll be home soon!" Vicky rubbed the gem again and Ursa disappeared. She sat down on the sand. Ursa had brought up Chaily. He had died unexpectedly, but Ursa said that they weren't telling anyone who wasn't on Sio. She said that

35

they didn't want to hinder any of their journeys, and they would let them know when they returned. She agreed that this was probably the best idea, but Lenna, Dimi, and Ruller will not be happy when they find out.

Vicky stared up at the mountain. A bird was circling it. It was an odd looking bird, and it was carrying something in its hand. She stood up and advanced forward.

"Birds don't have hands," Vicky said quietly. Suddenly, the bird turned. It swooped down and flew quickly along the side of the mountain. It was coming her way. The bird picked up speed, and soon Vicky could see its details. It wasn't a bird at all, but a boy. He had long, light blonde hair which was messy and wind-blown, and he was tall. He wore a large shirt with long, loose sleeves. It was white with a light gold trim, and it reached down to his knees. He also wore off-white pants which were very loose, and no shoes. Coming out from the back of his shirt was a pair of large, feathered wings which looked almost angelic. He was carrying a large staff in his hand. It had a brown shaft, and at the top was a large, diamond-shaped ruby with two spikes jutting out from the sides.

The boy was only a few feet away from her, and he lifted his staff and swung it at Vicky's head. She ducked at the last minute, successfully dodging. She turned and ran towards her ship. She sprinted across the sand, but then looked back. She could see the boy's eyes now. They were red. He pointed his staff at the ship and the ruby began to glow brightly in the sunlight. The spikes on the sides began to shine, pulling in the light. Vicky stepped forward but tripped over her feet and landed face down in the sand. She turned over and looked at the boy, who was hovering right above her, still pointing his staff at the boat. She stared at the glowing spikes, and then she saw the sunlight shift and shine directly into them. Small, orange beams appeared from the sunlight around the spikes and flew into them. The ruby began to glow brighter. Then, a light shined in the center of the ruby, and a bright yellow beam shot from the tip of the ruby and hit the boat, exploding it on contact. The shattered remains floated on the water, all ablaze. Then the boy glared at Vicky, pointing his staff directly at her forehead. It began to shine again.

"No! Stop!" she shouted. The boy glared at her, still. She moved a little to sit up, and he didn't move at all. Then she moved the hand next to the grappling hook around her waist. The boy jerked forward, touching the tip of the ruby to Vicky's forehead. The girl saw the beams appear from the sunlight. "No!" she screamed. She grabbed the hook and threw it to the side. "See?! I don't want to hurt you!" she shouted. The beams disappeared, and the boy backed away slightly, still hovering above her. "My name's Vicky," she said. "What's yours?" The boy raised an eyebrow at her. "Do you talk?" she asked. She lifted her hand and made the motion of a mouth opening and closing. The boy put his hand to his chest.

"Rui," he said. Then he pointed at her.

"Vicky," the girl answered.

"Vicky," Rui whispered. He floated down to the ground and sat. He patted the ground beneath him. "Cumber."

"Yes! So this *is* Cumber!" Vicky said. Rui stared at her. "Oops," she said. There was silence. "I like your wings." Rui stared at her again. She stood up and walked behind him. The boy's wings jerked up and he sprang into the air, pointing his staff at her again. "No!" She sat again, waiting. After a moment, he floated back to the ground. Again, Vicky walked behind him, and this time, she put her hand on his wings. "Wings," she said. Rui moved the tip of one of his wings to his hand.

"Wings," he said quietly. Vicky shook her head at him. She patted one wing.

"Wing," she said. She put her hands on both wings. "Wings." Rui repeated what she demonstrated. Then he picked up some sand. He held it up to Vicky and stared at her. His face suddenly looked curious, like a small child's. The girl guessed that he was fifteen years old. "Sand," she said. Rui sprang into the air and picked Vicky up, barely giving her enough time to pick her hook up from the ground. They soared over the land and up into the mountain. Rui placed Vicky on the ground at the mouth of a large cave. He waved his hands all around him. "Cave," she said. She walked around and pointed out various objects on the floor. "Stick. Fire. Log. Water. Bowl. Rock." The boy grasped the concept immediately, and he named off everything in the cave which

Vicky had pointed out. Then he walked out of the cave and pointed. Vicky looked out and saw that he was pointing at the half of the island which she couldn't see from the beach. It was entirely covered in trees. "Forest," she said.

Rui turned around and walked back into the cave. He sat down. "Rock," he said, patting the rock that he sat on. Then his stomach growled. He looked at Vicky.

"Hungry," she said. She looked around the cave. There was no sign of food. "Food?" she asked, making a motion as if putting something in her mouth, chewing it, and swallowing. Rui shook his head and frowned. Vicky clutched her stomach. She was hungry too. Rui stood up and pushed Vicky further into the cave. Then he held up his staff and began to move it around in a circle. The sunlight hit it again and it began to shoot its flaming beam. However, the beam didn't shoot outward this time. Instead, it expanded, forming a wall of fire along the entrance to the cave. Rui stepped back from it. He stared at the fire wall, nodded, and then walked back to where Vicky was. Then he lied down on the floor and went to sleep. Contrary to Rui's schedule, Vicky wasn't tired. After all, the sun was still out and she was focused on how much she still wanted food. However, she sat down as well and closed her eyes. It took her a while to fall asleep.

*   *   *

Rui shook Vicky awake the next morning. He smiled and pointed towards the entrance to the cave. The fire wall was still burning, and lying next to it was an animal. Rui picked up his staff and walked over to a cup of water sitting on one of the rocks. He held the staff over the water and waited. Soon the spikes began to glow, and small blue beams flew from the water into the spikes. The ruby began to glow, and then a bright blue beam shot out from it. Rui turned the staff towards the fire wall and quickly extinguished it. Then he walked over to the animal and hit it with the staff. It didn't move. Vicky stood up and walked over to where he was. The animal had scorch marks on its fur, clearly from jumping into the fire. It was dead. Rui took a knife from his pocket and began to cut up the animal.

Vicky turned away in disgust, refusing to look at the bloody sight. After a few minutes, Rui was roasting the meat over the fire. He handed a piece to Vicky, and hesitantly, she ate it. It was delicious.

After about an hour of relaxing, Rui stood up. He spread his wings and circled the cave, picked up Vicky, and flew out towards the forest. Rui brought them to the ground once again when they were in the middle of the trees. He stepped up to a tree and patted it.

"Forest," he said. Vicky shook her head.

"Tree," she said. Then she flung her arms up, waving at everything around them. "Forest!" Rui stared at her blankly for a moment, and then nodded his head. He flew up to the top of one of the trees and picked two apples off of its branches. Then he flew back down and held them out of Vicky. "Apple," she said, taking one and biting into it. They walked a few feet and arrived at a river. "River," Vicky said, pointing. Rui ran over and scooped some water from it.

"Water," he said, remembering the water from his cave. Vicky smiled and nodded. Suddenly, without acknowledging the presence of someone new, Rui took his shirt off and dunked it in the water. Vicky blushed and turned away, trying to give the boy some privacy while he washed. She stood with her back to him for a few minutes, and then it was her turn. She was given equal privacy. It felt good to be clean after the long ride on the boat.

The two friends walked through the forest, naming everything they saw. They walked for hours, and soon the sun began to set again. Rui picked Vicky up and flew out of the trees. When they left the forest, Vicky noticed that they were very far away from Rui's cave. The boy's wings batted the air. It was obviously a challenge for him to fly with the extra weight. However, they made it safely back to the cave just as the sky became dark. Rui picked up his staff and held it over the fire. Soon he had his beam firing from the ruby, and the fire wall was built again. Then he lied down on the hard ground and went to sleep. Vicky sat down too. The entire day she had been thinking about a problem that she needed to solve. Rui wouldn't be able to carry her all the way back to Sio, and he had destroyed her boat the previous day. How were they going to get back? Even worse, how would she communicate to him that she needed his help?

*   *   *   **

Vicky stayed with Rui on Cumber for eight weeks. Over that time, she was able to teach Rui a lot about her language, and he was beginning to be able to slowly form sentences without her help. One day, Rui had left the cave to find some food, but returned in a hurry.

"Vicky," he said, "what is that?" He pointed out to the ocean, and Vicky saw a small boat sailing across the water.

"Of course!" she screamed happily. "Rui, it's a boat. I had one too, remember?" Rui thought for a moment at what she said. "We have to signal it, it might be one of my friends!"

"Signal?" he asked.

"Shoot a beam towards it. Don't hit it," she instructed. Rui held up his staff, absorbed some sunlight, and fired a beam directly above the boat. However, the boat didn't come to them. "Rui, we have to leave."

"Leave . . . Cumber?" Rui asked, shocked.

"Yes," Vicky answered. "I have friends. They need help. Understand?" Rui thought for a moment, trying to understand what she said. Then he nodded.

"We will fly," he said.

"Can you carry me out there?"

"Yes." Rui extinguished the fire burning on the ground and then looked back at his cave. He frowned, and then turned to Vicky. He held his staff under his arm and picked her up. Then they took off. Rui carried Vicky over the island and out to the sea. They were about a half of a mile from the boat when Rui began to fly lower. "I can't," he said, and his eyes closed. They plummeted into the water.

"No! Don't give up!" Vicky said, worried. She swam over to Rui, keeping him above the surface. She could hear voices coming from the boat, but she couldn't understand what they were saying. She saw three figures come to the side, and then one jumped overboard. Vicky kicked harder, but her legs couldn't support the two of them. She tried to keep her head above the water, but she slowly began to sink. Then, something began to hold her up. She looked down at the water and saw a large fish three times her size swimming underneath her. She sat on the fish's back as it carried her and Rui towards the boat. Next to them, a small, purple fish rapidly swam. It seemed to smile at her.

They were at the boat in a matter of minutes.

"Nice of you to join us," said a familiar voice. Vicky stared up at the side of the boat and saw Dimi looking down at her. "Who's your friend?"

"Dimi!" she shrieked. "This is Rui! Help me up there!" The boy reached down and grabbed Vicky's hand. Rui slowly flew up to the boat's deck and collapsed. Vicky jumped up and hugged Dimi. "How did that fish know to save us?" she asked.

"Ask Vesa," Dimi answered. Vicky looked over the side of the boat at where the purple fish once swam. Now, a girl swam where the fish was.

"You're a fish?" Vicky asked.

"Yup!" Vesa answered. "I can communicate with other fish too. You're welcome."

"Vicky, I want you to meet Luc and Vesa," Dimi said. "Luc is our snake."

"It's nice to meet you!" Vicky responded, smiling at Luc.

"Help me up there!" Vesa called from the water. Dimi walked over to the side of the boat and held his knife over the side. It quickly extended into a long, wooden pole which Vesa then used to climb back onto the deck.

"This is Rui," Vicky said. "I can't really explain what he does ... But he flies!"

"He'll have to explain when we get home," Dimi said.

"Home," Rui said, sadly and quietly. He sat up and stared at Cumber, which was disappearing into the distance.

"Home," Vicky repeated. Ursa's face appeared in her mind.

Chapter 5:
The Spirit's Secret

The sun had almost set over the horizon when Sio came into view for Lenna's boat. Lenna and Divy stared at the approaching island. Tears were streaming down her face.

"Divy, it's horrible!" she cried. "Look at it!" She pointed at her home. What was once a welcoming landscape had turned to the exact opposite. Grassy lands with dirt patches and beautiful lakes were now covered by trees. In fact, the entire island was covered in a thick forest. In the center of the forest was a tall, black castle which loomed over the entire area. The mountainous northern edge of the island now sat in smoke. "That's from the three volcanoes. They're supposed to be inactive, but they must have opened back up."

"Is it safe for us to approach in the boat, or should we abandon it?" Divy asked.

"Let's abandon it while we're still a safe distance away," Lenna answered. "Lisha! Do me a favor?"

"Yes?" Lisha asked.

"We're abandoning ship. Set the boat on fire with me. Kita, Mira! Get ready to jump!" Mira quickly ran and retrieved all of their belongings and handed them to Divy. Lenna and Lisha stood next to each other. Lenna began to rub her hands together quickly, and soon small flames were shooting out. Lisha watched this, and then turned. She held her hand out and took a breath in. She puffed out and stiffened her hand. A ring of fire shot out and engulfed her section in flames. Lenna stared in awe at how easily this was done.

"I'll teach you," Lisha said, smiling. "Let's go!" They jumped overboard.

"Swim underwater!" Divy shouted. The five took in a breath and dove under. Divy took the deepest breath and then made a pushing motion once he was under. The underwater currents shifted, and the five were sent tumbling towards Sio. They were soon on the shore, gasping for air.

"Thanks for warning us!" Kita said.

"You're fine," Divy answered, straightening up and tossing her her bag.

"I'm so sorry you all have to see Sio this way. It's not supposed to be this . . . unbecoming," Lenna said.

"It's fine," Mira responded, "just lead the way to your hideout."

"If I can find it," Lenna said quietly to herself. She had no idea how they would get around in this new setting. "Hold on," she said. She walked over to a tree with low branches and began to climb to the top. She scanned the area. "I know where we have to go!" she called down. Then she jumped down, falling over her long skirt, and began to lead the way.

The group walked for hours through the trees. By now the sun had completely set and everything was dark around them. Lisha held up a small flame, lighting the way. They were walking very close to each other.

"Wait," Divy said. A twig had snapped somewhere. Everyone stood still. Lisha dropped her hand, extinguishing her flame and placing everything into total darkness. Something moved behind them.

"Get in a circle," Lenna whispered. The five stood back-to-back, ready to fight. Something jumped from a tree overhead. "Who's there?" Lenna called out. There was no answer. She turned her head slightly. "Everyone stay ready—"

"Look out!" Lisha shouted. She swiped her hand in front of Lenna and a stream of fire shot out. Their attacker was illuminated.

"Wait!" Lenna screamed, spreading her hands into the flames. The fire disappeared right before it touched their enemy. "Lisha, give me light!" The area around them lit up, revealing a young girl standing a few feet in front of Lenna. She was fourteen years old and had long brown hair that hung over her shoulders. She wore entirely black clothes with a long, black, hooded cloak. Her fists were raised, ready to strike. She stared Lenna down at first, but then her face softened. "Ellia?" The girl stared at Lenna, and then smiled widely.

"It's you!" she screamed happily. "Okay, wait here!" She smiled and waved. Her body began to glow a bright indigo color, and then she was sucked backwards through the trees.

"Who was that?" Kita asked.

"It looked like Ellia, but I've never seen her so happy," Lenna answered. "And how did she disappear so quickly like that?"

"Hey, she's *your* teammate," Lisha said. "You tell us." Someone stepped through the trees.

"Lenna?" asked a voice. Ellia stepped back out, only less expressive this time.

"Ellia!" Lenna said happily.

"Lenna!" Ellia ran and hugged her friend. "Come on, this way." The girl began to lead them through the trees. "Who are you all?"

"Ellia, this is Divy, Lisha, Kita, and Mira. What was that?" Lenna asked.

"I have a new power!" Ellia exclaimed. "I can make copies of myself, but of course there's a catch. Each copy is given only one emotion, and as long as that copy is free, I can't feel that emotion at all. I would say I was sad without happy Ellia, but sad Ellia is out scouting the other side of the island. Actually, hold on, I want to be whole again." Ellia stopped walking and closed her eyes. She took a deep breath, and her skin began to glow indigo. Something flew through the trees and into her body. Her glow brightened and then faded. "Sorry about that. It's a really useful power; now I know everything that my copies saw and encountered while they were out. Quick, we need to get inside. There are spirits around." Ellia began to run and the five others followed. They stopped next to a large rock. "Would you like to let us in?" she asked Lenna.

"It *has* been a while," Lenna answered. The girl stepped forward and touched the rock. When her hand made contact, the rock opened and revealed a staircase.

"Everyone inside, quick," Ellia said. They climbed down the stairs and into a dark hallway. There was a dim light shimmering at the end, and Lenna began to sprint towards it. Finally, she entered the Circle Stone Room.

The room was just as she remembered: large and circular with a table-like stone in the middle. This was the Circle Stone. There were nine people in the room when she arrived. One was a twelve year old girl with short black hair who was wearing a sleeveless shirt, a skirt, and black shoes. This was Ursa. Next was Ruller, talking to three people who Lenna didn't know yet. Then there was Shenny, who was exactly like Ellia in age and appearance except she wore a long pink dress with long, loose sleeves. She had an apron tied around her waist and her long brown hair was tied in a ponytail. Next to her was Sensho, the only adult in the group. Sitting on the ground was Grev, a fifteen year old boy with a shaved head, tan skin, a tan, sleeveless shirt, and brown pants with brown sandals. He was sharpening a sort of spear that had a sharp point at the end and a blade like a sickle coming out from the tip. He used a rock to sharpen it. Finally, there was a nineteen year old girl with pale skin dressed entirely in black. She wore a thick belt which had multiple bombs attached to it. Her deep black hair was up in two messy buns, one on either side of her head, and she wore a golden bracelet which took up most of her left forearm. Decorating the bracelet were seven gems, one for each member of the Circle Stone Group, and a black gem on the opposite side.

"Lenna!" Ursa screamed when she came in. The small girl ran over and almost tackled her. The quiet room was filled with noise as everyone rose to greet her, and finally, she called for silence.

"Everyone, I want you to meet Divy, Lisha, Kita, and Mira. Divy can control water, Lisha controls fire, Kita controls earth, and Mira controls air. They're our new friends from Ixie!" Everyone cheered at Lenna's successful trip, and the group from Ixie was officially welcomed to Sio. "Now, there are three people I don't recognize, and one who has a story to tell. Ruller, how was Helite?"

"It was great!" the boy answered. "We got back about . . . eight weeks ago, I think. This is Maura, Kit, and Maia. Maura is a shape-shifter, Kit turns objects into different objects, and Maia can turn invisible and open portals to different places. We came back using Maia's portals on the day I met them. Also," he began to whisper, "Kit doesn't speak our language very well. Maia and Maura can, but that's because Maia learned it and Maura turned herself into someone from Sio. Kit's been learning from a book he has."

"I am learning!" he said defensively. He stepped towards Lenna and thought for a moment. "My name is Kit. I am from Helite. It is very nice to meet you."

"Hello, Kit," Lenna answered. The boy smiled at his success.

"I'm Maura," Maura said, stepping forward and waving.

"And I'm *Princess* Maia," Maia said, forcefully.

"Princess?" Lenna asked. "Well it's nice to meet you." She turned to Maura. "Is she going to be a problem?" she whispered.

"I'll take care of it," Maura answered. Then she turned around. "It's called humbling yourself," she whispered to Maia.

"I don't have to humble myself to anyone," she responded.

"Make sure to tell me how that works for you," Maura replied, walking away.

"Where's Chaily?" Lenna asked, looking around. The room became silent.

"Oh . . . he's out scouting the island," Ellia replied. "Just seeing what Gabent's up to and such." She turned and sat down next to Grev. "Change the subject!" she whispered.

"Not one of your best ideas," he whispered back. "Careful. So Lenna, did you have a safe trip?"

"Yes, for the most part. There was a storm right before I made it to Ixie, but other than that it was safe."

"You were caught in that storm too?" Ruller asked. "It must have covered the entire ocean! My ship was destroyed in it!"

"You too? How did you survive?" Lenna asked.

"My book's been showing me new spells lately. I made a shield around myself and floated some of the way. The rest was luck."

"That's great! I'm happy you're okay." Lenna looked at her friends happily. She had missed them more than she thought. "What happened to the island? Where are all the towns? I didn't see a single person while we were walking."

"Oh, it was so scary," Shenny answered. "You see, since you all left, we've been leaving this room more often. We have to find our own food and clothing, after all. We can't wear the same thing everyday! I'm sure you noticed Ellia's cloak, we only wear those when we leave. Anyway, it was right after you left that it all happened. Meemee and I were outside sneaking around and looking for some food when Gabent let his spirits loose. They entered into every town and destroyed every building that was still standing. Whatever people were hiding were taken to the castle, because you know that most people were taken when Gabent took over to begin with. Then he rose over the mountains and struck the three volcanoes open. It's amazing that they didn't erupt. Then the rivers and lakes ran dry, even though they're still connected to the ocean. He must have set up a spell, the water just stops where it should be entering. Everything was covered in small trees after about a week. Fortunately, sneaking around has been easier, but it's hard to find food without going all the way up to the mountains."

"Do you think he knows we're alive?" Lenna asked.

"Probably not," Shenny answered, "but you never know. He could be watching us right now."

"Though it is extremely unlikely," Sensho said. Divy yawned after hearing this. "And it seems like now is a good time to end this conversation. It's also a good time to make some bedrooms for everyone. I'm sorry to ask you this, Lenna, when you just got back, but we need your help. What was your name? Kita? Will you and Lenna please make some rooms for everyone? We have all this space underground, I don't see why everyone shouldn't have their own room."

"Sure," Kita said, stepping forward. She and Lenna walked to a part of the wall.

"Let's have some organization," Sensho said. "We'll have separate sections for each group. First, the Circle Stone Group. Make an opening leading to a hallway, and then seven openings for seven rooms."

"Six!" Ursa interjected. Ellia glared at her. "Uh, Vicky and I will share a room." Kita stood in front of Lenna and placed her hands on the wall. She stepped back and thrust her hands forward. The wall moved backwards, forming a long hallway. Lenna and Kita stood on opposite sides of the hall and pushed the earth back, forming three rooms on each side. The only difference between the rooms was that Lenna's were circular while Kita's were square. They stepped back into the Circle Stone Room.

"Now do the same for Shenny, Meemee, Grev, and me, and so on for everyone else." The two girls followed the same process, and soon they sat on the ground, tired, staring at their work. Everyone now had a place to call their own.

"Have you all eaten today?" Shenny asked, stepping up to Lenna.

"We're fine, thank you," Lenna replied. "We ate just before we arrived."

"And we each have plenty in our bags that we packed for the trip," Divy added.

"Blankets?" Shenny asked.

"We have those as well, thank you," Mira answered.

The warriors said good night to each other and retired to their bedrooms. Everyone had been given a blanket by Shenny despite their refusals. She had been working hard making them with the limited tools that she had.

"Ellia," Lenna said before stepping into her room, "when's Chaily going to be back?"

"Oh, um, he should be back tomorrow," Ellia answered quickly. She stepped into her room.

"I've really been looking forward to seeing him," Lenna said.

"Lenna . . ." Ellia began. She couldn't bring herself to tell Lenna the bad news just yet. "He'll be back tomorrow."

"Great, thanks! It's great to be back here with you!" Lenna said, leaving the room. Ellia was left by herself. She had been leaving the Room more and more since Lenna left, and with using her new powers everyday, she'd begun to exhaust herself. She sat on her bed and prepared for the night. She didn't have time to settle in, though, before two other people walked in.

"Excuse us." Ellia turned around to see Mira and Divy standing in her doorway.

"Oh, hi! Is everything okay?" Ellia asked.

"Well," Mira answered, "we don't know you that well, but we've been feeling like something's wrong here. Is everything alright?"

"Everything's fine," Ellia said. "Should it not be?"

"We were just concerned," Mira said. "It must just be us, then. Have a good sleep! Come on, Divy."

"You too!" Ellia said as they exited. Mira and Divy walked back towards their rooms.

"Well?" Mira asked. Divy held up his hand and revealed a small drop of water floating above his palm.

"It didn't swirl once," he answered sadly. "She lied to us."

*   *   *

The next day brought cold into the Circle Stone Room. The change of seasons from summer to autumn had begun, and everyone crowded around a small fire.

"We need more fuel to burn," Grev said. "Lenna, come with me to cut down trees."

"Sure," Lenna said. She stood up and followed him.

"Take this," he said, passing her a cloak from a pile on the ground.

"Thanks," she responded. They donned their cloaks and walked out of the room and into the forest.

"Stay low," he said, "there are spiders in the trees."

"Normal spiders or Gabent's spiders?"

"Both, and I can't say that I like either of them." He began to crawl along the ground, dragging his spear behind him and stopping every now and then to look up into the trees. "Think you can cut trees down?"

"I've never tried," Lenna answered, "but it's worth a shot." She stood up and faced one of the trees. She opened her hand and sliced into the trunk. She screamed in pain.

"Quiet!" Grev said, jumping up and covering her mouth.

"It didn't work," she pointed out, her eyes tearing. "Hold on." She extended both hands towards the tree. Focusing, she moved one up and one down. Slowly, the fibers of the tree expanded and snapped, making it fall and take down three other trees with it.

"Get down!" Grev ordered. He fell flat on his stomach and waited. Lenna fell next to him and didn't move. Something snapped. "Get behind me!" Grev shouted, standing up and twirling his spear around them. A giant spider came walking through the trees. It snapped its massive pincers at them, but Grev stood his ground. "Get back to the room and get Ruller."

"I'm not leaving you alone with this thing," Lenna answered.

"Go! I can fight it." Lenna ran off and back through the rock entrance, down the staircase, and into the Circle Stone Room.

"Ruller! Grev said to come get you. Hurry up!" The small boy jumped up and grabbed a cloak. He put it on as they ran out.

"What's going on?" he asked, frantically.

"Grev's fighting a spider. He said for me to come and get you."

"Did you cut down some trees?"

"Yes, but that's not the point!" Lenna turned and saw Ruller walking.

"Don't worry, he's fine. He wants me there to help bring the trees back."

Lenna stopped running as well, but continued walking quickly. "He can't fight it by himself!"

"Yes he can, I've seen it. Look!" Ruller was pointing at Grev, who was hacking away at one of the trees with the curved end of his spear. The spider's corpse was on the ground next to him.

"Oh, Ruller. Help us bring these back." He grunted and swung one more time. The tree came toppling down, bringing four more with it.

"*Thera!*" The trees shrunk into the size of pebbles, and they picked up each one and carried them back.

"Grev, what's that?" Lenna asked. He was carrying a small sack that he didn't have when they left the room.

"Oh, it's the spider's web sack. Shenny uses the web material inside to make these cloaks. It's really strong."

"You mean I'm wearing parts of the spider?!" Lenna shouted. "Tell me you're joking!"

"Nope!" Grev smiled and continued walking. Soon they were back at the Room.

"Look what Kita made!" Divy said. He was holding something made of stone in his hand, but they couldn't see what it was in the dim light. "It's a torch holder! We can have more torches burning along the walls!"

"That's great!" Ruller said, walking over to look at it.

"Ellia, the sun's high in the sky. When will Chaily be back?" Lenna asked.

"Umm . . . later." It sounded more like a question than a statement.

"Okay no, that's it! You can't do this, Ellia!" Grev said suddenly.

"What are you talking about?" Lenna asked.

"Chaily's not coming back," Grev responded. There was silence. Everyone was now listening. "He died."

"What?" Lenna asked quietly. Her eyes began to fill with tears.

"Grev, you're telling her wrong!" Shenny said, pushing him aside and running to comfort Lenna. "Let her know more kindly!"

"She should've been told the moment she got back!" he answered.

"No, stop this," Lenna said, her voice cracking. "This isn't funny. Whose idea was this? Where is he?"

"Lenna, it's not a joke," Ellia answered. "I was just waiting for the right time to tell you." Lenna pushed Shenny away from her and ran out of the room.

"She can't be outside!" Shenny said. "She can't be seen, someone has to go after her."

"Well I'm not going," Maia said loudly.

"No one asked you to, Princess," Divy responded. "I'll go." He grabbed one of the cloaks, put it on, and left the room. When he stepped outside, he noticed that the sky was darkened with clouds, even though Lenna had just said that the sun was out. Somewhere close by a trail of rain was falling into the trees. He went to it and found Lenna sitting on the ground, drenching herself in water. He raised his hand and stopped the downpour.

"Leave me alone," Lenna said through her tears.

"Stand up," he said. The girl ignored him. "I'm not letting the rain fall until you stand up and do as I say." She rose and looked at him. Her eyes were red and puffy. "You're hiding your tears by soaking yourself in water, but your eyes are giving you away. Take a stance. I want you to take the rain drops and put them together into a stream of water." He dropped his hand and the rain began to pour down. Lenna lifted her hands and moved them together, bringing the rain into one large drop. Divy pulled the water from her and made it circle around her body. "Drink some of this," he said, stopping the water next to her hands. Lenna cupped her hands and Divy filled them. She drank silently. Divy started to move the water around her once again. "You were really close to Chaily? You definitely had feelings for him, and he had them for you too. You were devastated leaving him to go to Ixie, but you made sure he stayed here in order to protect him, correct?"

"How do you know all of that?" Lenna asked. Her eyes followed the water as it circled her.

"I'm good at figuring people out. Stop the water and disperse it onto the ground." Lenna raised her hand over the water and waved it towards the ground. The stream separated and was quickly absorbed into the grass beneath them. Divy sat down and looked at the grass. "Without that water the grass would die, and without the grass the animals would have nothing to eat. If you think about it, you just helped to save many lives. After all, living things are part of nature too, right? I know it's a bad example, but I guess what I'm trying to say is that when something bad happens, something good happens in return."

"I looked forward most to seeing him once I got back. Catching up, showing what we've learned, and making a new plan to save Sio. Now that's all gone." Lenna stared at the ground.

"It's not all gone, though. You can still make a new plan and you have all of your friends here to help you through it." He stopped speaking. "Someone's coming." The boy looked behind him. "Get down!" he shouted, pulling Lenna down to the ground. A bright blue beam shot through the trees. Divy turned his back and held up the side of the cloak. It was hit, but no damage was done.

"How do you know that these things will work?!" Lenna asked, panicking.

"I don't." Divy turned around, extending his arms out, closing his fingers, and pulling back. The air in the distance suddenly became liquid, and the water came rushing towards them. A spirit was being pulled along with the water. "Help me out!" he said, turning to Lenna. "There's water in the air. Use it!" Lenna swung her arms in a circle and a stream of water appeared from her fingers. She shot it at the spirit, covering it with a large wave. Then she lifted the water up, carrying the spirit with it, and closed her hand. The water froze instantly, and the spirit was trapped inside. "Did that thing send that bolt?" Divy asked.

"I don't know," Lenna answered. "I've never seen that happen before."

"What is it?"

"A spirit," Lenna answered. "They serve Gabent."

"It's kind of scary. I didn't see that face a minute ago." Divy was peering into the ice.

"They don't have faces. They don't even have bodies. They're just dark cloaks," Lenna said, turning towards him.

"Well look at this one." Lenna looked at the cloak inside the ice. An old and wrinkled face was glaring from under the hood. She stepped back in fear.

"He's all skin and bones!" Lenna exclaimed. "He looks dead!" The frozen face continued to look out from inside the ice. "Do you think he's alive?" At that moment, the ice around the spirit's hands began to shine brightly. Divy's face became serious. He pushed Lenna back and stood in front of the ice. He was nodding his head as if he was counting. Then, he raised his hands and closed them into a tight fist. The ice shattered, and the spirit shattered as well. The dark cloak and the man inside were completely destroyed. "What did you do?"

"I froze the ice," he answered. "The spirit isn't alive. If he were alive, he wouldn't have been able to use his powers. When you freeze something, all of its muscles stop, including its heart and brain. The spirit would have blacked out if he were alive. You're correct in saying that he's dead, which I guess clarifies why they're called 'spirits'."

"So he's undead?"

"Pretty much. We have to tell everyone about this." Divy turned and began to head back to the Circle Stone Room. Lenna followed at his heels.

"What do you mean, you 'froze the ice'?" she asked.

"I mean that I froze the ice," he said, walking quickly. "I saw the beam growing from his hands. He was going to shoot it out and break the ice around him. I waited for the perfect moment, and then froze the ice even more than it already was. He hit himself with the beam."

"How do you make ice more frozen? That's not even possible. Once it's frozen, it's frozen," Lenna debated.

"Not if you keep it in its place. Maybe that's the correct explaination. I kept it in its place." He walked up to the rock which hid the entrance to the Circle Stone Room. Lenna stepped forward and placed her hand on it. The staircase appeared, and the two walked down into the Room, where they found everyone sitting in a large circle. "We found stuff out about the spirits. Apparently, they literally are spirits. Dead people. At least that's what we think."

"And they can shoot beams at us now, too," Lenna added. She sat down between Maura and Lisha.

"You were seen?" Ellia asked, worriedly.

"Yes, but we killed it," Divy answered.

"You killed the dead thing?"

"Yes." There was silence as everyone tried to figure out what Divy was talking about. They gave up after about a minute.

"So how about making up a new plan?" Lenna suggested anxiously, trying to smoothly break the silence.

"Lenna, we need to apologize . . ." Ellia began.

"Don't," Lenna said. "I don't want to talk about." Silence again.

"We don't have everyone else with us to make a plan," Grev finally said. "Shouldn't we wait until Vicky and Dimi get back before we start anything?"

"I guess so," Lenna said. "Then everyone start to think of a plan in the mean time, okay?" There was mumbling amongst the room. Maura was translating to Kit, the group from Ixie had begun to whisper to each other, although it looked more like they were gossiping than thinking, and Ellia was drawing in the dirt with her finger. Everyone, for the most part, was eager to accomplish this new task.

*   *   *

When evening arrived and everyone retired to their bedrooms, Lenna found herself unable to settle down to sleep. She was sitting on her bed when Shenny and Meemee walked in.

"We want you to know what happened to Chaily," Meemee said. "We were with him when he died." Lenna stared at them, waiting.

"Right after you all left and Gabent took over," Shenny explained, "Meemee, Chaily, and I went into the towns to find surviving people. We knew that the towns were deserted, but we wanted to be sure of it. We were in your town, Sheno Village, when it happened." Tears had begun to build in her eyes, so Meemee took control of the conversation.

"We were trying to lay low because the trees hadn't grown yet, and so Chaily ducked behind a bush. He called us over to where he was. On the ground next to him was the body of a man who had passed away. We couldn't figure out how he had died, but we assumed that it had happened during Gabent's takeover and his body had just been left there. Chaily reached down to examine it, and then he just collapsed. The second he touched the man he was down."

"His body glowed orange," Shenny quietly added.

"Oh, right," Meemee said. "When he died, his body glowed orange for a second, and then it died down. We buried him in that spot. Everyone came out for the burial, despite the risk of being seen."

"We all hoped it wasn't true," Shenny said. "We hoped he had passed out or something, but he wasn't breathing and his heart had stopped. He was gone. We just wanted you to know the story. You have the right to." There was silence and tension in the room.

"You all could've been seen," Lenna said. "You should've buried him here."

"We didn't want to have to hide the fact that we lost one of our own," Meemee explained. "It was a matter of pride, I think."

"Thank you," Lenna said, dismissing them. The two girls left, leaving her alone. The image of Chaily stayed in her mind as she fell asleep, and a bright orange light filled the sky in her dreams.

Chapter 6:
A New Plan

The groups adjusted easily to living with each other. Friendships were made with only minor disturbances to the peace of the Circle Stone Room. Maia began to argue with Lenna and Sensho over who had authority, but she was pulled aside by Maura before anything drastic happened. The members of the Circle Stone Group who had stayed on Sio seemed to have become sick of living with each other, but it was assumed that that was only because of the conditions. Also, everyone noticed how all of the girls seemed to flock towards Divy; sitting on his lap, laughing whenever he made a witty statement, and linking their arms into his whenever they walked anywhere. Of course, he didn't complain about this attention at all. Only Lenna, Meemee, and Maia kept out of his way. Of course, they liked to sit and talk with him, but they weren't looking for anything more than to be just friends. On the other hand, even the youngest, Ursa, didn't want to be separated from him.

The daily schedule consisted of four main activities: searching for food, observing the comings and goings of Gabent's castle, training, and leisure. Jobs were appointed to different people each day, but there were also the usual few who did the same thing everyday. Shenny continued to make clothes, Grev, along with whoever he chose to accompany him, went out in search of food and firewood, Ellia led the team of "castle watchers", as they had come to be called, and whoever was left without a job sat in the Room and trained or made it more liveable. Sensho had taken to making beds for everyone from the firewood that Grev brought in, but this was difficult due to his lack of supplies. Kita was usually good to force a stone nail into the wood to keep it together, though. Mattresses, pillows, and blankets were stuffed with whatever they could find, which was usually just leaves or grass. Every now and then, a bird was brought back from the mountains, and its feathers were plucked to stuff the pillows, its meat was cooked and eaten, and its bones were made into whatever tools they were good for. No one liked having to work this much in order to survive, but they did what was needed.

One week after Lenna had arrived back from Ixie, the door to the Circle Stone Room opened. It was nighttime and everyone was eating, so no one noticed it at first. In fact, even as the intruders entered the room, they still were unnoticed. Finally, one of them spoke.

"So this is the welcome we get. We've been gone for how long, and all you do is sit there and eat?" Everyone turned around, faces full, and stared in the direction that the voice came from. Standing in the hallway were Vicky and Dimi, smiling happily at their friends. Behind them stood Vesa, Luc, and Rui.

"I'm hungry," Vicky said, stepping forward. She sat down next to Ursa and took the meat that was in her hands. She began to chew it while smiling at her sister, whose jaw had dropped at the sight of her. Finally, Ursa screamed with joy and tackled her sister. At the same time, Ellia stood up and jumped into Dimi's arms. Everyone then scrambled to greet their friends and meet the new warriors from Paro and Cumber.

"How did you get here at the same time?" Meemee asked.

"Dimi found me and Rui when he was passing Cumber on the way back," Vicky answered.

"More like they dropped in on us," said Dimi. "I looked over the side and I saw the two of them flying towards us."

Once everyone had been introduced and finished eating, Kita and Lenna made another hallway with five rooms for the group from Paro, and one doorway leading to Rui's room. "Good," Sensho said, supervising their work. "Move whatever spare beds we have into the rooms, and all of you go to bed." The man stood up and went into his room. The rest walked to their assigned bedrooms.

Ellia stepped into Dimi's room. "Chaily's dead," she said to him. "We don't know how or why, but he's dead. That's why he's not here. Ursa's telling Vicky. I just wanted you to know before something bad happened."

Dimi was quiet for a moment. He stared at Ellia, then at the floor, and then back at Ellia. Then he asked, "How did Lenna take it?"

"Horribly, but Divy helped her out."

"The water-boy? It's interesting that a newcomer would know how to help her."

"He was with her traveling for eight weeks; it makes sense that they grew close. That's more time than we've even spent with her. I was surprised that he was so quick to volunteer, but he's really a nice boy and really fun to be with. I hope you two can get along." Ellia turned and began to leave.

"Wait, Ellia." Dimi stood up and grabbed her hand. He kissed her on the cheek. "I've grown close to Vesa and Luc, too. I think they're rubbing off on me." He turned her around and led her to the hallway. She silently walked back to her room. No one saw her giant grin or dark red face.

*   *   *

The next morning was probably the easiest morning that the groups had since they arrived on Sio. Ruller was the first one to rise, as usual. He stepped outside of the Room to see what the day was like, only to find that the sun was already high in the sky. Everyone had slept through the entire morning, and once they were all awake, they were happy to have slept late. Next, now that Vicky was back, she and Ursa could conjure whatever food everyone wanted to eat, as long as it wasn't too heavy for the both of them to carry. The groups decided to have a feast to celebrate the safe arrival of Dimi and Vicky.

Once everything was cleaned up, it was time to improve the housing situation even further. The blankets, pillows, and mattresses that weren't very comfortable were thrown into a storage room that Kita formed in the wall. Maia stepped up and recommended bed coverings that were fit only for the highest of royalty. Once they were conjured by Vicky and Ursa, everyone silently agreed that this would probably be the only time that Maia would be useful to them.

Along with improvements on the beds, the girls were also able to bring forth some furniture as well. Chairs with soft cushions appeared in their hands, and materials for sofas and tables appeared as well. Sensho taught the boys how to put everything together. He was surprised that none of them knew how to build a simple table. As well, the boys were able to put together some chests to hold everyone's clothing.

Rugs were spread across the floor, and the Room was divided into different sections. There was a long table with twenty chairs around it, a large cooking pot, various cooking utensils, and a large fire sitting on one side of the room. This was the area for cooking and eating. Another section had a large map of Sio from before Gabent's takeover posted on the wall. It displayed the vast mountains all the way to the north, Mount Cris in the center, grasslands to the west, desert to the south, and barren land to the east. Beaches lined the edges. There were also stacks of large paper sitting on top of a long desk. This was the planning area. A large portion of the room was given to a training area. This area had no rug, but was paved over with stone to provide for a better training ground. It was set up so that two of the warriors could spar in a generally safe environment. Finally, a soft rug was placed underneath various couches and pillows. This was the leisure area, and it was seen as a mandatory requirement by Divy.

Three days passed before everything was perfect. The groups were working fast and were soon able to sit down in the leisure area and breathe a sigh of relief. It was then that the different friendships really appeared. Although everyone sat together talking, it was obvious who was friendlier with whom. Shenny, Lenna, Meemee, Mira, and Sensho were one small group, having mature conversations about life and other various subjects. Another group was Divy, Rui, Kit, Ruller, and all of the girls. Although the girls liked to go and visit with groups having deep conversations and expressing opinions, it seemed that those boys were the most fun to be with. They were the easiest to speak to out of everyone, and as friendships grew, it was easier for everyone to get along. Finally, there were Dimi, Grev, and Luc.

The boys would constantly move around playing pranks on the other warriors and making jokes. No one was annoyed, though. Some of the jokes they came up with were very entertaining, and everyone liked a good laugh. The only person who didn't belong to a specific group was Maia. She would travel from group to group, turning the conversation towards herself and trying to be the center of attention. She always failed.

On the fourth day, Sensho confronted Lenna. "Isn't it time to come up with your next strategy? You've brought these children here and uprooted their lives. You should focus on taking back Sio in the fastest and safest way possible."

"You're right. What would you suggest?" she asked him.

"If I were in your situation, I would call aside the leaders from each group. They will tell you what will be the best suited plan for their fighters."

"Okay, I will." Lenna stood up and called everyone to attention. "Can you please separate into your individual groups? Circle Stone Group, come over here with me please. Ellia, I need your help." Ellia stood up next to Lenna.

"Oh yeah," Maura interrupted. "Ruller, you said you would think of a name for us, but I think I have an idea! We'll be the Changing Group, because we can each change something." She pulled Kit and Maia close to her.

"We'll be the Animal Group!" Vesa shouted. Luc, who did not see the need for names but did not want to anger Vesa, was nodding in agreement.

"And we can be the Elemental Group!" Divy said.

"Rui," Rui said quietly, smiling.

"Okay . . ." Lenna said.

"Wait!" Grev said. "Me, Shenny, Sensho, and Meemee need a name too."

"But you're all part of the Circle Stone Group," Vicky responded. "Remember? Sio said you could . . ."

"True, but we're not. We have no powers. We'll be the Human Group," Grev answered.

"Fine, you all have your names," Ellia said impatiently. "Lenna?"

"Thank you," Lenna said. "Now that we're all here and settled in, we need to start thinking of a new strategy. Instead of having everyone shout ideas at once, it would probably be best if the leaders from each group came with me and Ellia so we can make a simple but effective plan. Can all of the leaders please stand up?"

Immediately, Luc stood up. Everyone stared at him.

"What? I'm obviously the leader of the Animal Group," he said.

"Don't get too full of yourself," Mira and Divy whispered simultaneously.

"Luc, you're strong, but you're also an idiot, and you tend to overreact," Vesa explained. "Our leader is the smartest and most balanced of all of us: Feo. Don't think that you get bumped up just because he's not with us."

"Feo?!" Luc shouted. "He's insane! Balanced? Absolutely not."

"Sit down," Vesa said, standing up and pushing Luc to his knees. She walked up to Ellia and stood next to her.

Maura stood up next and approached Lenna. There were no objections. Rui, who had been listening to Vicky slowly explain what was happening, stood up next and walked over to the other leaders. There was silence from the two remaining groups.

"What's the problem?" Lenna asked.

"We don't know who our leader is," Shenny answered. "We always followed you and Ellia."

"Well, who would come up with the best plan?" Ellia asked.

"I would, of course," Grev answered.

"The last time we let you come up with the plan, we were almost killed by the people in Fort Aras," Ursa said.

"Meemee is our leader," Sensho said.

"Why?" Meemee asked.

"You have the universal communication between the Circle Stone Group and our group. Also, you coordinate yourself well with others and adapt to every situation. You are our leader." Sensho stared at her until she stood up with the others.

"And what's going on over here?" Ellia asked, turning towards the Elemental Group.

"We want Divy to be our leader," Kita explained, "but he refuses to get up."

"Why?" Lenna asked.

"Because Mira's older than me and more mature," he answered. "She should be the leader."

"However," Mira added, "I'm not comfortable being leader and I would much prefer if Divy was."

"Well, one of you has to help us," Ellia said.

"Just go," Mira said to Divy. He stood up and joined the rest.

"Good. The rest of you can continue relaxing," Lenna said. She led the group of leaders over to the map of Sio. Ellia sat down at the desk and began to draw on a piece of paper with a writing rock. After a few minutes, she had a new map of Sio drawn. This one displayed the island with its trees, mountains, and Gabent's castle.

"Okay, this is our current island," she said. "What are your ideas?"

"Gabent's inside the castle," Maura said. "We have two choices. We can either get inside and find him or we can figure some way to destroy the castle from the outside, bringing him down with it."

"We can't get this many people into the castle without being noticed," Vesa said.

"First, let's think about what we have to risk," Divy said. "There are no other people on the island, correct?"

"Not that we know of," Ellia responded. "We've been around the island dozens of times and have never seen anything more than spirits or spiders."

"So it's only our lives that are at risk? Great," Divy said. "We can work without having to worry about anyone else being caught up in it."

"Let's focus on something from the outside," suggested Vesa. "It needs to be powerful, though; something more than just knocking it down."

"Of course," Maura said, "that would be too easy. What can we do that will ensure that everything inside that castle is destroyed. What are our resources besides our powers?"

"None," Lenna said. "Look at the map. We have trees, ocean, and mountains. That's it. We need to rely on our powers alone for this."

"Not necessarily," Ellia said, separating and walking to the map of Sio from before Gabent took over.

"Crush him," Rui suggested.

"Lisha!" Ellia called.

"Yes?" Lisha answered.

"Come here for a minute." Lisha walked over to Ellia. "Can you move lava?"

"No, lava isn't fire. It's melted rock."

"Okay, thank you. You can go back to the others. Kita, can you come over here?" Kita stood up and went to Ellia. The other leaders had stopped making suggestions and were now staring at her. "Can you move lava?"

"I guess that I should be able to," Kita answered. "I've never tried before."

"Okay, thank you. You can go back." Ellia turned to the leaders. "I have an idea. There are three volcanoes in the mountains. We send Ruller to one, Lenna to the second, and Kita to the third. From there, they move the lava out of the volcanoes and onto Gabent's castle. Gabent will be killed as the castle is destroyed!"

"What if he teleports away?" Meemee asked.

"He won't see it coming! He thinks we're dead!" Ellia responded excitedly.

"Won't the entrance to this room be covered by the lava?" Divy asked. "And what if there are spirits in the mountains? And can Ruller, Lenna, and Kita really move all of that lava by themselves?"

"Ruller can," Lenna answered. "He can just cast his levitation spell and move it that way. It's me and Kita who actually have to use our energy."

"If there are spirits then the three of them can just kill them," Ellia said.

"I think that other people should go into the mountains with us just to be safe," Lenna said.

"Fair enough," said Ellia. "Ruller and Maia can transport the people up there. Is that okay?" She turned and walked back to the others before any of the leaders had a chance to respond. "Okay," she announced, "we have our plan. We're going to burn down the castle! Lenna, Ruller, and Kita will travel up to the three volcanoes in the mountains. They will then force the lava to rise out of the volcanoes and travel down to Gabent's castle. It will be destroyed, and he'll be killed as well."

"That's a good idea," Shenny said. "He never leaves the castle."

"Won't the lava run on the ground, though?" Dimi asked. "It'll block out our entrance."

"That's what I said," Divy said, sighing and sitting down next to him.

"Lenna and Kita can just move the lava away from the entrance later," Ellia said.

"Like they'll know where it is," Divy added spitefully.

"We'll figure it out," Ellia said. She turned to Lenna, Ruller, and Kita. "So, the three of you can bring some people into the mountains with you, just to make sure you're safe. Pick who you want." Ruller called over Ursa and Vicky. Lenna walked to Divy and grabbed his arm, and Kita pointed at Lisha. "When would you all like to go?"

"So you brought all of us here for nothing?" Luc suddenly interjected.

"You're not here for nothing," Ellia answered. "We can bring you right back to Paro when this is finished."

"Couldn't you have figured this out sooner, and then the rest of us wouldn't have had to come here?" Luc responded.

"Shut up!" Vesa commanded, slapping him on the back of the head. "I have a question that I hadn't asked before. What if Gabent catches us and comes out of the castle?"

"I was wondering that as well," Sensho said.

"If that happens," Meemee answered, "I can help coordinate a response with everyone here. We can move out quickly, as long as someone makes sure that there's no lava around the entrance."

"We can handle that," Lenna said. "Let's get it done now. We wouldn't want to keep everyone away from their homes for too long." She looked at Luc, who Vesa now had in a headlock. Despite her small size, she could easily handle him. Lenna then looked over at Sensho, who was nodding. "Maia, please help transport everyone to the volcanoes."

"Why can't Ruller do it?" Maia objected.

"Because it will be done faster if you help, now open up a portal and send me and Divy to one of the volcanoes," Lenna answered.

"Don't they have names?" Maia asked. "This would be easier if I knew where you were going."

"Nope, so figure it out."

"Wait!" Shenny said. "Before you leave, make sure to put these on for protection." She handed each of them a cloak. They put them on and then stared at Maia.

The princess stood up and stretched out her arms. She tore open a portal and thrust her hand inside of it. Her whole arm was illuminated with a bright green color. She turned to the others. "It's ready. Lenna and Divy go first, then Kita and Lisha." Lenna climbed into the portal and was followed by Divy, who was slightly hesitant. Maia put her hand into the portal again. When she removed it, Kita and Lisha jumped in. Maia released the edge and it snapped shut.

"Why did you keep putting your hand in it?" Vesa asked.

"I have to make sure it's going to the correct place."

A voice came from Ruller's spell book. It was Lenna. "Ruller, are you ready yet?"

"We haven't left yet. I'll let you know," he said to Lenna's gem. Vicky and Ursa grabbed his hands. *"Anla fro Circle Stone Room portran volcano!"* They disappeared.

*   *   *

Ursa and Vicky reappeared at the top of a large mountain. They were standing on an extremely narrow strip of land, and right below them was the crater of the volcano. They could see the bubbling lava below. It was a long drop down.

Suddenly they heard a loud, ear-splitting scream. Ruller was tumbling through the air. His spell had failed to place him on the land, and so he appeared over the open crater. Vicky and Ursa, wide-eyed and scared, watched him fall.

"Rili!" he screamed. Nothing happened. *"RILI! RILI! RILI!!!"* The girls could hear him crying as he desperately tried to cast his spell. At one point he stopped, but he failed to float higher

into the air. Tears were forming in the girls' eyes. Vicky threw her hook down after him, but it couldn't reach. Ruller was a small distance from his death. *"BUFAS!"* he screamed. Bright violet energy formed a round shield around him. He floated in the lava. *"RILIIII!"* he sobbed. The lava around him began to levitate, and he was soon engulfed in it, his force field keeping him safe. His book began to glow, and it opened up to a blank page. He could barely read his new spell through his tears. From the surface of the volcano, Vicky and Ursa looked down upon the faint violet glow coming from underneath the lava. Ruller pointed a finger to the top of the force field. He knew that once he cast the spell, his protection would disappear. *"Transfer Vicky!"* he sobbed. A violet light appeared in his chest. It ran throughout his whole body until it reached his finger. Then it shot out, breaking the force field. The boy was swallowed by the lava.

Ursa and Vicky watched the violet light flicker away. As their tears fell down the crater, Ruller's spell burst out of it. It swirled towards the girls and flew straight at Vicky, colliding with her heart.

"Vicky!" Ursa shouted, making sure her sister wasn't hurt. The girl had begun to glow bright violet, which slowly changed to green. Then she was normal again. "Are you okay?"

"Fine," she croaked. "I'm fine." She collapsed onto Ursa, and they both laid there crying.

Two volcanoes away, Lenna stood in position. She removed her headband and rubbed Ruller's gem. "Get ready," she said, staring away from the blank gem and into the volcano.

"Lisha," Divy said into his necklace. Lisha's face appeared in the gem. "Tell Kita to get ready. Lenna, are you ready? Go now!" Lenna swung her arms towards the crater and brought them back over her head. The lava within began to rise, and she repeated the process several more times. Soon the lava was rushing over her head and down through the mountains. "Watch where you're sending that stuff," Divy said, dodging the edge of the flow.

"Sorry," she answered, continuing to pull the lava up to the surface.

"I can see Kita's trail. It's moving quickly," Divy stated.

"Can you see Ruller's?"

"Not yet, maybe he's too far away." Divy stared at Kita's work. Then, something about the area changed. "Do you feel that?" The ground had begun to shake. The lava was rushing towards the top of the volcano.

"That's not me making that happen!" Lenna exclaimed. Divy spun around, making a trail of water appear from his hand. He shot it towards a nearby mountaintop and froze it in the air. He kept one arm raised and crossed to the mountain.

"Come on! My arm's getting tired!" Lenna slowly advanced across the ice, being careful not to slip. When she made it safely to the other side, Divy dropped his arm. The ice trail fell and shattered on the side of the mountain. "Always remember that there's water in the air," he said. Then, the volcano began to erupt, shooting lava from the top.

Lenna stomped her foot on the ground, forming cracks underneath them. Then she bent over and lifted her body up again. Four walls grew around them, pushing their bodies together.

"This is cozy," Divy said, raising his eyebrows. "You made this tight on purpose, didn't you?"

"Oh yes," Lenna smiled, "I just wanted to be near you." She kissed him on the cheek and laughed.

"You are a tease," the boy said, laughing. "Make a hole in the wall so we can see out." Lenna pressed her fingers into one of the walls and pushed. Part of the wall crumbled and a hole large enough for them to see out of appeared. The lava was rushing through the mountains. It was beginning to burn the trees down by the castle.

"This is great!" Lenna said. "It's going fast enough that it'll take the castle down the moment it hits it! Kita's trail is already combining with mine. Do you see Ruller's yet?"

"No, not yet," Divy answered. "I wonder what's taking him so long. Look! It's at the castle!" The lava was a few inches away from the base of the structure. They could see the edge coming closer and closer to the castle's walls. Then, a black light surrounded the building. The lava was pushed to the side and continued to travel around the light. The trees were burnt down as it spread out across the island. When it reached the water, it stopped. Lenna and Divy stood with their jaws dropped. Lenna pushed the walls down and looked out at the castle, protected by its dark force field. "Of course," Divy said. "This plan was too easy." He rubbed the gem on his necklace. "Mira." Mira's face appeared. "Please ask Maia to bring us back." A few seconds later, the portal appeared at their side and they stepped in.

"How did it go?" Ellia asked when they appeared on the other side.

"He had an invisible force field up the whole time. It appeared when the lava hit it. The castle still stands and now the trees are gone. We can't leave here anymore," Lenna explained. Kita and Lisha stepped out of their portal.

"Well that was a big waste of time," Kita complained.

"Really?" Divy remarked.

"Ellia," said Vicky from her gem on Ellia's clothing. She was speaking softer than usual. "We need Maia to open a portal for us." Maia opened a portal and Ursa and Vicky stepped out with tears still running down their cheeks. They were soaking wet.

"Aw, it's okay," Shenny said, hugging them. "We'll get them next time. Has it started raining outside? You're both all wet."

"Those aren't normal tears, Shenny," Divy said, breaking them apart. "Where's Ruller?"

The two girls burst out crying again. Their whimpers were heartbreaking. "He fell into the volcano!" Vicky said loudly. She and Ursa ran to their room. The room was silent. Lenna's eyes began to water, and she ran off to her room. Shenny sprinted away as well. Everyone else in the room turned to Sensho for consoling. They sat down and listened to his words of comfort while Divy and Mira strayed away from the group.

"You go see Lenna," Mira said. "I'll go to Ursa and Vicky."

"What about Shenny?" Divy asked.

"Go to her after Lenna. She's a big girl, she can last by herself," she said. Divy walked into Lenna's room. She had her face buried in her pillow and her long hair was askew. She looked up at Divy. Her eyes were bloodshot.

"First Chaily and now Ruller!" she gasped. "He was so little! And he was the most powerful of all of us!"

"I know," Divy said. "He was a good kid. He was smart and was always looking out for everyone." Lenna turned over and continued to sob into her pillow. "Remember back on Ixie when I told you that we had five entrances to our secret room, but there were only four people in our group? There's actually a fifth, but he died."

"What happened to him?" Lenna asked, wiping her nose on her sleeve.

"We were training one night and he wasn't being careful. He fell off of a mountain that Kita brought up from the ocean. He broke his back as he fell and then drowned. His name was Ery. Lisha took it the hardest. I didn't really mind him being gone. You can say I'm a bad person for that, it's okay. I agree. I never really cared when anyone died. I know that they're dead, so what's wasting my time worrying about it going to accomplish?"

"Where are you going with this?" Lenna asked, confused.

"After Ery died, we all had to cope without him. He was a really good friend of mine, and now I will never see him again. I know one thing, though. He wouldn't want me grieving over him. He'd want me to move on and learn to live my life without him. That's what he'd want from Mira, Kita, and Lisha, too." He moved his hand up and pulled a small stream of water from the air. He led it with his finger towards Lenna and made it circle around her head. Then he brought it back and began to make it float between his hands. "So I practice my powers and learn about them. There's water in the air and every living thing. It's in the sky, the ground, and of course, the oceans. I need to make sure that I can compensate for us not having the extra person. Kita and Lisha will never put in the effort. They're too spoiled. Mira tries, but if she makes a mistake, she loses confidence and stops."

"Kita and Lisha don't seem very spoiled to me," Lenna said.

"Give it time. Give them one situation where they don't get their way. Did you ever notice how Kita will always interrupt someone if she has something to say? Usually everyone just disregards it. Eventually it gets annoying. And Lisha is just lazy. But they're not the point. The point is that Chaily and Ruller wouldn't want you wasting your time crying over them. They'd want you to be sad, but work to improve. Ruller died trying to help us, he wouldn't want everyone to stop now." Lenna sat up and smiled.

"You're right. What was Ery's power?" she asked.

"He controlled empty space."

"What's that?"

"The fifth element that few people recognize. It's difficult to explain, and also difficult to use. Basically, it's everything in between what holds things together. So, he can control basically anything. Or he can in theory, anyway. We didn't really have much time to experiment. We were practicing the night he died. Do you believe that there are other planets besides ours?"

"Stranger things have happened."

"They exist, and they are separated by an area that has no air, water, fire, or earth. *That* is empty space. People are made up of it, too."

"You're really smart, did you know that?"

"No I'm not," Divy said. "I just observe things."

Mira walked into the room. "Can you two come to Vicky and Ursa's room?"

"What's wrong?" Divy asked, getting up.

"Ursa's really sick." They walked into the girls' room. Vicky was kneeling next to Ursa's bed. Mira had changed them both into dry clothes.

"What's wrong with her?" she asked. Lenna walked over and put her hand on Ursa's forehead. It was hot, and the girl was in a cold sweat. She was shivering under her blankets. Her eyes were closed and tears were leaking out from under her eyelids.

"I think that she caught something while she was in the mountains," Mira said. "Has she ever been up there before?"

"Just once that I know of," Lenna answered. "Unless you count all the times she's been up Mount Cris; in that case, then yes, many times. Vicky, please go get Sensho. He'll know how to help." The girl left the room in a hurry. She returned moments later with Sensho at her side. He bent down over Ursa, felt her forehead, her pulse, and listened to how she was breathing.

"She needs to stay in bed," he said. "Her body is under so much stress that it can't fight off the illnesses around her. I've seen this before. It's fatal if not handled correctly."

Chapter 7:
A New Book and New Weapons

"Fatal?!" Vicky shouted. "It can't be fatal! Help her!" Tears were beginning to form in her eyes once again.

"I'll do what I can," the man assured her. "She should be fine. Lenna, please take Vicky away from here so I may work." Lenna took Vicky by her hand and walked out of the room.

"So what can you do for her?" Divy asked.

"Nothing," Sensho replied. "I can make a medicine that will bring down her fever and fight off whatever is inside of her. However, I cannot guarantee she will recover." He shook Ursa's shoulders. Her eyes slowly opened up. She groaned. "Ursa, where are you hurting?" She put one hand on her forehead and another on her stomach. "That pain will extend to her legs and arms, and she won't be able to move soon," he told Mira and Divy.

"Maybe I can help," Divy said. He placed his hands over her forehead and separated them. A wave of water appeared between them. He placed his hand on her forehead, making sure that the water stayed there to keep her cool.

"It won't work," Sensho said. "The pain can't be relieved until her body learns to overcome it." The boy dropped his hands to the side and the water disappeared into the air.

"I'm going to the others," Mira said. She stepped out of the room, heartbroken at the thought of the helpless girl being tortured by something she might not be able to fight against. When she stepped into the Circle Stone Room, she found Shenny and Grev staring each other down and Lenna trying to push her way between them. Everyone else was sitting off to the side, afraid to interfere. Mira sat down next to Maura.

"What's happening?" she asked.

"They're arguing," Maura replied. "Grev told Shenny to toughen up and that she's acting ridiculous for crying over Ruller. Then he said that she didn't really contribute to the groups at all. He said that someone who only sits there and makes clothes all day is just one more mouth to feed."

"Was he trying to comfort her?" Mira asked.

"I think so. Anyway, Lenna's trying to calm them down."

"Both of you stop this," Lenna was saying. "Shenny, you have no idea how important to us you are. Grev, apologize. You're wrong."

"Apologize?!" Grev shouted. "Why? She's getting angry over nothing! Besides, I'm right and you know it!"

"No, you're wrong," Lenna said. "Shenny cooks, makes clothes, helps everyone, and fights with us."

"Well we can't have her sitting around crying, and we can't have you sitting around crying either!" Grev said. "She's worthless like that! At least you have your powers to substitute for your poor leadership skills."

"So what you're saying," Shenny interrupted, "is that you would all be better off without me?"

"Yes, I am," Grev answered.

"Fine!" she shouted. She turned around and walked to her room, quickly returning with a cloak in her hand. She held it tight around her and walked out of the room and into the hallway that led to the staircase out.

"Shenny!" Lenna shouted. "Shenny, come back!" She ran down the hallway after her.

"How will she leave?" Dimi asked. "Aren't we buried under here now by the hardened lava?"

"Yes, we are," Lenna said, returning, "but somehow she figured out how to leave. She just disappeared when she got to the top of the staircase. See that?" she asked, turning to Grev. "That's someone we needed! Even more, that's someone from *your* team! From *our* team! That's not how people are supposed to treat each other!"

"You're really stupid sometimes, Grev," Ellia said, standing up.

"Don't call me stupid!" he shouted back, advancing towards her.

"Don't get any closer!" Dimi said, standing up.

"Everyone just calm down!" Lenna said, but Grev shoved her out of the way.

"I agree with him," Maia said, standing next to Grev and glaring at Lenna. "It's time we had a real leader around here."

"Because you're a real leader?" Maura asked, standing up next to Dimi.

"She'll be a better one than you," Luc said, arriving at Maia's side.

"Think realistically, Luc," Vesa said, joining Maura.

"Come on, can't we all calm down?" Lenna tried to ask, but she was once again shoved out of the way.

"Didn't you hear her?" Mira asked, shocked.

"Vesa, you're not exactly the best of all of us," Lisha said. "You can only do something when you're in the water. At least we can be useful no matter where we are."

"All you do is visit Luc every night, and we all know what goes on then," Kita added.

"What goes on between the two of them is their business!" Meemee said, protecting Vesa.

The room was suddenly filled with shouting. Grev and Dimi had become violent and were hacking at each other's weapons. Lenna turned to Kit and Rui for assistance, but they were too confused by their language barrier. She ran to them, but was too scared to say anything. Everything was falling apart. Vicky ran to one of the tables and began to throw various cups of water at Luc. Kita and Lisha had turned on Vesa, and Kita held her as Lisha prepared to strike. Mira was screaming over the roar for everyone to stop. Meemee and Maia were touching noses as they screamed in each others faces.

Everyone was too distracted by what they were fighting for to notice Divy reenter the room. He had a serious face on as he took in what was happening.

"I leave the room to comfort someone and take care of a sick girl and this is what happens?!" he shouted. He stepped back with one foot and swung his arms towards the ground. He then raised his hands high and let loose a long breath. A tall wall of ice grew from the air and water which Vicky had thrown on the ground. It separated the mob into two sides. Grev and Dimi were thrown backwards as it grew under their feet and Kita and Lisha were forced to back off of Vesa. Meemee, who had hung onto the wall as it lifted up, was now on her back after falling. The room was silent, and everyone was staring at him. "I don't know if you know this, but a nine year old boy just died by being burned to death. There's now a twelve year old girl in the other room who's so sick that she can hardly move and you're all out here at each other's throats. Everyone sit down and calm down!" he ordered. All except for Grev and Dimi sat.

"Why should we?" Grev objected.

"Ever since you showed up," Dimi said to Divy, "you've acted like you're the center of attention and kept all the girls at your side. You act like you're so tough, but all you are is a skinny little annoyance! Do you ever stop?"

"I told you to sit down," Divy said. "I don't think you realize this, but I have no problem hurting you. I had respect for you, but now I've lost it."

"Well, I owe you no respect at all," Dimi said, pushing Divy's shoulder. The room was silent. "And you really think you're stronger than us? We're bigger than you; you have no chance."

"Listen to me," Divy said. "Sit down, both of you." Grev stepped behind Divy and grabbed his arms. The water-warrior didn't struggle, but merely stared at Dimi. He raised an eyebrow at him, as if daring him to lift his weapon. Dimi did. Divy jumped up and fell to the ground, breaking Grev's hold on him. From the ground he kicked Grev's shin, causing the boy to fall. He crawled to the side, avoiding Dimi's slashing knife. Grabbing Dimi's wrist as it came towards him, Divy stood up and bent it backwards. The boy yelped in pain, and he knelt down. Just to show how he wasn't going to show anyone mercy, he kicked both of them in the side.

"Anyone else want to step up?" he asked, staring down the room. He was answered by silence. The boy raised his hand towards his ice wall and brought it down. The wall liquefied, splashing everyone except for Lenna, Rui, and Kit. "What's this fighting about? Where is this coming from? Do you really think it will solve your problems? Let me remind you again that we now have two comrades dead, and judging by the fact that I don't see Shenny, I'm guessing that one of you messed up and now has to pick up the pieces. I'm not going to point any fingers," he said, looking at Grev, "but I have a pretty good idea who this was. Everyone say good night and go to bed. We'll deal with each other tomorrow calmly."

With that, everyone got up to leave. Divy stopped Maia and Maura as they walked past him. "You two are helping me clean up. Nothing personal, you're just the first two people that I could grab." He stepped away and began to pick up the cups which Vicky had thrown. Lenna approached him.

"How did you do that?" she asked.

"The ice wall? Lift up the water and freeze it," he answered.

"No, how did act like that?"

"Let me guess," he said, "you tried to vocally calm them?"

"Yes."

"Doing that is bad because no one will hear you. When I walk into a room, everyone is going to do what I want the way that I want it. Want to know what doesn't make spoiled? I'm open to doing what other people want, and most of the time I just want to keep everyone happy. In this case, they were going to do as *I* said. Grev and Dimi were the idiots. Sometimes you have to hurt people to get a point across, and the fact that I hate all of you helps me to show no mercy to anyone."

Lenna hesitated. "You don't like us?"

"I don't like anyone, it's just my attitude." Lenna didn't know if she should be offended or astonished.

"You didn't even use your powers, though," she said.

"No one said I needed to," he answered. He turned to Maia and Maura, who were finishing cleaning up the sitting area. "We're done. You can go to bed."

"Finally!" Maia said. "You know, Divy, you should just take charge all the time. You would make everything easier."

"Please don't start," Maura began.

"Go sit in your room," Lenna said.

"No. I think it was established already that I don't have to listen to you. Nice job solving those problems." Lenna's face instantly became serious. She didn't need to look at Divy for approval. She turned around, stomped her foot on the ground, and extended her arms. Pulling them back to her and closing her hands into tight fists, two columns of stone lifted up from underneath the unsuspecting princess. They encased her hands, raising her up high into the air. The expression on her face was that of terror. Lenna thrust her hands towards the ground, lifting herself up on a small tornado. She stared Maia straight in the eye.

"I am the leader of the Circle Stone Group," she said. "This is my island, this is my base, and you are now one of my warriors. You will show me the respect that I deserve." A trail of flames had begun to creep up to the trapped girl.

"Okay!" Maia whimpered. Lenna sank to the floor and nodded her head. The columns shattered, causing Maia to drop.

"Sleep well," Lenna said to Divy and Maura. She disappeared to her room.

*　　　　*　　　　*

Ursa was groaning in her sleep. The noise woke Vicky, and she sat up and looked at her frail sister. Their room was completely dark, but she could tell that Ursa looked worse than before. She turned her back to her sister and stared at the wall. Her eyelids began to close. They were almost shut when she saw a faint green light appear towards the bottom of the wall. She sighed heavily. The last time a green light appeared at her bedside, it was an orb which brought her to Mount Cris and started this battle with Gabent. Right now the last thing she wanted was for a new adventure to start. She stared at the light. It was small and dim. Suddenly, another light appeared, and then another after that. Four green lights arranged in a square were glowing from the bottom of her wall. Confused, she rolled out of bed and walked towards them. She extended her hand out. They were coming from something leaning up against the wall. Vicky felt the object. Her fingers ran over paper and then down a rigid spine. It was a book. She picked it up and felt along the wall until she found the door. She advanced down her hallway and into the Circle Stone Room. There was a single torch burning on the wall, giving the room an eerie glow. She opened the book to see what was inside.

Vicky stared at the text before her. She quickly closed the book and grabbed the torch off of the wall. She ran into Lenna's room and lit the torches hanging on her walls. Then, she shook the girl awake. Lenna groaned.

"Vicky?" she asked, sleepily. "What's wrong?" Vicky held the book in front of Lenna's face. "What's that?"

"A book," Vicky answered. "Open it and look inside." Lenna opened up to the first page and looked at the same symbols that Vicky had.

"What do these mean?" she asked.

"I don't know, but they're the same symbols that were in Ruller's book!" Vicky exclaimed.

"Sshhh," Lenna said. "You don't want to wake up everyone. Are you sure these are the same?"

"Positive. Ruller showed me them the night that we all met, and I've seen them every time I've looked at his book. I don't know what they mean, though." Lenna flipped through the pages. Just like with Ruller's book, this book had a series of blank pages in the back. When she arrived at the back of the book, she found the legend of Sio illustrated on the pages.

"You're right, this is like his book," she said. "What's this?" She turned past the legend and looked at the remaining pages. On the left page there was a picture of a tall boy with curly black hair. He had a sad face and pale complexion. At his side was a long sword. There were more symbols underneath the picture.

"That looks a lot like Chaily," Vicky said.

"It does," Lenna whispered. "We need to figure out what these symbols mean." Vicky took the book from her hands. She turned to the pages in front and looked at the symbols on each one. Finally, she pointed to a set of them.

"These are on every page," Lenna said. She indicated this combination: |●| ◻ ⬙ ⊓ ⊓."Five symbols means five letters, right?" Vicky nodded. "These probably stand for 'spell' since this was a spell book. For now, let's assume that." She turned back to the first page. "Ruller was looking at this page the night we all met," she said. "It was the summoning spell, remember?"

"He took Ursa's gloves," Vicky said.

"Right! So then these must mean 'summoning'," Lenna said, pointing to the |●| ◇ ◺ ◺ ⊓ ⋁ ⊓ ⋁ ▣ combination. "And then these at the bottom must be the spell."

"So then these must mean 'coget'," Vicky said, pointing to the ⊠ ⊓ ▣ ⬙ ◿ combination. "So then we have the symbols for S, U, M, O, N, I, G, P, E, L, C, and T. Let's figure out the rest!"

"I think we should get some sleep, first," Lenna said, yawning. "Go on, we'll figure this out tomorrow." Vicky nodded and left the room. She lied down in her bed, clutching the book close to her chest, and closed her eyes. As she faded in and out of sleep, the mysterious alphabet danced around her mind.

*　　*　　*

Everyone was shocked the next morning when Vicky told them the story of how the book appeared in her room. Her story distracted them from the riot of the previous night, although Grev was constantly being shoved out of the circle formed around Vicky. As she tantalized the room with her tale, Lenna, Sensho, Vesa, and Kita made a chart of the letters which they knew in an attempt to decode the book.

C - ⊠
E - ⬙
G - ▣
I - ⊓
L - ⊟
M - ◺
N - ⋁

O - □
P - ◙
S - ▣
U - ◩
T - ◪
' - ^

They looked at the inscription under the picture of the boy who looked like Chaily. From it they were able to translate: T◙e S◩o◪◩sm◙n Gu◙◪◩s T◙e ◪◙◪◪ L◙n◩s.

"Well that doesn't make much sense," Vesa said.

"This is too annoying," Kita whined.

"No, look at this," Sensho said. "What is a three letter word which begins with 'T' and ends with 'E'?"

"The," Lenna said.

"I think that it is safe to assume that we have two 'the's' in here. Therefore," he pointed at the ◙ symbol, "that stands for H. So overall we have, 'The something something the something something'." He turned the page back to the pages with the spells written on them. He stopped at the one of the most recent spells to appear in the book. "This is Ruller's fire spell," he said.

"How do you know?" Vesa asked.

"It's the only spell that he has which has a four letter word before the word 'spell'. The word goes, 'symbol-I-symbol-E', meaning that the first symbol is F and the second symbol is R. Do we have either of those letters?"

"Yes," Kita answered. "We have R." She had written the inscription on a piece of paper and proceeded to make the appropriate corrections. The sentence now read, "The S◩or◩sm ◙n Gu◙r◩s The ◪◙r◪ L◙n◩s."

"Can you figure out anything else?" Lenna asked. Sensho's eyes flashed back and forth as he looked from page to page. He stared at the sentence again. Lisha walked over from the group to speak with Kita.

"How's it going?" she asked

"We're stuck," Kita answered. Lisha looked at the sentence that Kita had written down.

"That word is 'guards'," she said, pointing to the paper.

"How can you tell?" Sensho asked.

"Can you think of any other word that fits?" Lisha answered. "Try it." Kita picked up a writing rock and filled in the letters which matched the symbols. "I think she's right," she said. "Look at the sentence." It read, "The S⊔ordsman Guards The Dar⊠ Lands." Lenna stared at the picture for a moment. The other four leaned in and waited for her to say something. Then she gasped in excitement.

"It IS Chaily!" she exclaimed happily. "The Swordsman Guards The Dark Lands!"

"I don't get it," Kita said.

"The Dark Lands are what people here on Sio call the afterlife!" Lenna exclaimed. "That must be why Chaily died! He was supposed to!"

"Okay," Vesa said, "but why is that important?"

"It means that Chaily is in the Dark Lands," Lenna answered.

"Well if that's the afterlife, then of course he is," Kita responded.

"This text means nothing to us," Sensho stated. "It will not help."

"Are you sure?" Maura asked. The five reading the text jumped in surprise at her voice. She stared at them, smiling. "Do we have any food? Everyone's hungry." It was then that it finally hit them that Shenny was gone. She had always made sure that the groups were well fed. Lenna walked over to Vicky and pulled her to the side.

"Do you think you and Ursa will be able to conjure us some food? I'm worried that it will make her situation worse," she said.

"It only takes one of us to decide the item we conjure. Let me try," Vicky answered. She walked into her room and grasped Ursa's hand. Although she had her gloves on, her hand was cold, and Vicky could feel it through her gloves. "Bread," she said, separating their hands. A large loaf of bread appeared between them. Ursa's eyes slowly opened.

"Vicky," she mumbled.

"Go back to sleep," Vicky answered. "I didn't mean to wake you. I'm sorry."

"Vicky," Ursa whispered, "I don't like this anymore. I want to go home. I want it to stop. This isn't fun anymore." She began to whimper and cry. "I don't like this at all."

"I know you don't. It'll all be over soon."

"Please, make it stop. It hurts to be here. Everything hurts," Ursa sobbed. Vicky stared.

"Please," Ursa cried quietly, "make it go away. Make everything go away. I want to go home!" She closed her eyes again. Her breathing was shallow, but then changed to deep breaths. Tears ran from her face. Vicky stared at her, unable to breathe. She sat in silence, staring at her weak sister. Slowly, Ursa's eyes opened one more time. "Where's Ruller?"

"He died," Vicky answered. "He fell into the volcano."

"We didn't get to spend enough time with him."

*   *   *

Lenna walked up to Ellia who was speaking with Maura and Kit.

"What are we going to do without Shenny?" she asked.

"Look on the happy side," Kit answered. "It is one less person to be eating."

"I think what you mean is to look on the bright side and it's one less mouth to feed," Maura corrected.

"I am trying," Kit shrugged.

"We need to either find her or cope without her," Ellia said.

"How can you say that?! We *have* to find her!" Lenna said.

"How?" Ellia asked. "We can't leave here; there aren't any trees to cover us. From now on, anyone who goes outside will be seen."

"Then we won't leave here," Maura said. "A snake and a bird will." Lenna stared at her for a moment.

"I get it!" Lenna said. "Luc! Come here!" The boy walked over.

"We need your help," Maura said. "The two of us are going to look for Shenny. You need to be your animal when you leave here, though."

"That's fine," Luc said. "Oh, what about Maia? She can be invisible."

"She won't go and I don't want to deal with her," Maura answered. "Lenna, I don't know how Shenny got out before, but if the entrance is concealed, will you let us out?"

"Sure," Lenna answered. Before they could leave, though, Vicky walked out of the hallway to her room with a pile of food in her arms. "I think we should all eat first, though."

Rui and Meemee walked over to Vicky and took some of the food from her.

"How is Ursa?" Rui asked.

"No better than before," Vicky answered.

"Things will get better," Meemee said. Vicky smiled at her and then walked over to the table and set her food down.

"Okay," Vicky said, "what do we do now?"

"I can cook a little," Meemee answered, "and I feel bad bothering anyone to help us. If Shenny can cook for a group of people this big by herself, I'm sure that three people can figure out how to do it." She picked up a knife and began to cut up some vegetables. Rui took the meat and began to cut it up.

"Wait, what are we doing?" Vicky asked. "Hold on." She ran into her room and returned with a piece of paper. "I conjured us a recipe. Why didn't we think of this before?" She read off the directions which Meemee and Rui quickly obeyed. After an hour they had enough food prepared for everyone to eat heartily. The groups sat down at the table and began to eat.

"This is great," Kita said to Lisha. "As long as we have Ursa and Vicky, we live a better life than we did before."

After the meal, Lenna escorted Luc and Maura down the hallway to the exit.

"How does this usually work?" Luc asked.

"Usually we just put our hand to the ceiling and the exit opened," Lenna answered, touching the ceiling. Sure enough, the exit opened just as it usually did, only with more stairs to climb in order to get to the top of the now solidified lava.

"Let's go," Luc said, bending over. He quickly shrunk into a long, green snake with two large fangs extending out of his mouth. He slithered up the stairs and out of the hallway.

"We'll see you later," Maura said, jumping into the air and flying out. Lenna watched as a beautiful crimson bird soared out to the sky. Lenna walked back into the Circle Stone Room and joined the others.

"We can't keep this up," Ellia said to her when she sat down.

"What?"

"Losing! We try to win, but we lose, and if every time we try someone dies, we're going to run out of people!"

"Then we need to do something different this time; something completely out of the ordinary from what we usually do."

"What else can we do?" Ellia asked. "We've tried attacking directly, we've tried attacking indirectly, what other kind of attack is there?"

"I don't know," Lenna answered. She thought of the first time that they ever faced Gabent. They would have won if it wasn't for the amount of spirits attacking them. Or maybe she was just in denial, and they had no chance to begin with. Either way, they lost. "You know what I just realized?" she asked Ellia.

"Tell me."

"We have no idea why Gabent is doing this," she said. She looked at Ellia who had a confused look on her face.

"You're right," she said. "We never thought to find out. We were told he was bad and we had to stop him, but we had no idea why he was so bad."

"If we find that out," Lenna said, "maybe we can trap him in his own plan!"

"How do we do that?" Ellia asked.

"I have no idea," Lenna answered. She stood up, walked to the desk, took a few pieces of paper and a writing rock, and went to her room.

"What do you think she's planning?" Vicky asked Ellia.

"I don't know," Ellia replied. "She seems to have some kind of idea." Neither of them knew that Lenna was actually sitting in her room with her head in her hands waiting for an idea to come to her.

Hours passed, and the two searching for Shenny were out the entire night. The next morning, as everyone was waking up, a distress call was made.

"Maia! Maia!" A distressed voice was calling the girl's name. Maia was sitting with everyone in the Circle Stone Room, except for Lenna, who was still confined to her bedroom. Maia slipped her headband off and looked into one of the gems.

"What is it, Maura?" she asked.

"Someone needs to let us in," Maura answered. "Luc was attacked by an animal. He's hurt."

"Oh no," Vesa said, standing in a panic. "Sensho, please let them back in."

"What's going on?" the man asked, escorting Vesa down the hallway.

"Luc has a condition," she answered. "When he bleeds, he doesn't stop. He almost bled to death once."

"I know what to do," Sensho said. He pressed his hand to the ceiling and the entrance opened up. Maura jumped down with Luc in her arms. They rushed back into the Circle Stone Room and laid him down on the Circle Stone. Everyone gathered around to watch. Sensho tore open Luc's shirt, revealing the boy's chest, which was deep red.

"What happened?" Vesa asked Maura.

"We were near the mountains and another bird was in the sky," Maura answered. "It dove down and hurt Luc before we even noticed it."

"Dimi, give me your knife," Sensho said. The boy handed the man his knife. Sensho took a bottle out of his pocket and poured its contents onto Luc's body. The boy was not moving. His eyes were closed and he looked almost dead. Sensho pierced Luc's side with Dimi's knife, releasing a stream of blood from his body. "I need cloth!" Meemee ran over to the kitchen, grabbed a towel, and handed it to Sensho. He pressed down on the incision. Then he took the knife and made another cut, releasing more blood. He pressed down on the new opening. "Okay good, it's clotting," the man said. He pressed down one more time on the cuts. Luc's eyes jerked open and he gasped.

"It hurts!" he shouted, clutching the towel.

"Good, hold that there," Sensho said. "Divy, please?" He held out his hands. Divy brought forth some water and drenched them. "Thank you. Does anyone else want to share about any dangers they may have in their body so that we can be prepared for this?" He stared down the kids, who looked at him blankly. "Good."

"I think that we need to help protect them," Rui slowly said. "They need weapons. They cannot always fight as animals." He turned to Vicky to make sure that he had said everything correctly, and she nodded in approval.

"So we'll figure out a way to make weapons for Vesa and Luc," Meemee said.

"I already have my weapons," Vesa said. She pulled her knives from under her skirt.

"You've had those the whole time and didn't tell anyone?" Kita asked.

"I didn't feel the need to," Vesa answered. "Can you make a weapon for Luc, though?"

"Yes, why don't you make it?" Mira said to Kita. "What's a sword but melted stone?"

"Okay," Kita said, slightly hesitant. "What should I make?"

"Whatever he wants, or whatever you think would be good for him," Mira answered. She brought Kita a writing rock and a piece of paper. "We'll help you if you need it."

"If I can just see Grev's spear and Dimi's knife for a little while, I should be able to come up with something. May I have your knives, too, Vesa?" Kita asked. The boys and Vesa handed her their weapons. She observed them for a moment and then began to scribble on the paper.

Soon, Kita opened a hole in the ground and was sending rocks hurdling back to the Circle Stone Room. Lisha kept a steady and strong flame on them, causing them to melt into an easily bendable form. Once she was done, Kita had chains flying around the room and blades sharpening themselves against one another. Everyone who was there had to duck in order to avoid being hit.

"I'm sorry!" Kita said. "This is the easiest way to get things done quickly!"

After a while, Lenna stepped out of her room to see what the commotion was all about. As she entered the room, Kita almost hit her in the face with a chain that she was swinging around to make sure that it would hold strongly.

"Sorry, Lenna!" Kita said.

"It's okay!" Lenna said. She ducked down and crawled to join everyone else. "What's she doing?"

"Making Luc a weapon to protect himself," Meemee answered.

"Here," Kita said, handing Luc two circular shields attached by a tight chain. "You need the most protection. These shields can strap to your back and the chain will make sure they don't separate. They can protect you from most weapons and the sides are sharp enough to cut through stone walls. I think they'll cut through armor, too." She then turned to Vesa and handed her two hooked sheaths she had fashioned from thin stone. Her knives were already inside of them. "They're built to sharpen your knives every time you pull them out. I thought you might like these. I'm hungry." She turned to everyone else, and Vicky ran into her room to conjure another recipe. Luc and Vesa thanked Kita for their new weapons and immediately ran to the training area to test them out. Everyone else split up and returned to what they had been doing before Kita began making the weapons. Lenna returned to her room, Meemee and Rui went to the kitchen to wait for Vicky, and Sensho followed Luc to the training area in order to make sure that he was alright to fight.

When Vicky stepped out of the hallway to her room, her eyes were watering.

"What's wrong?" Maura asked.

"Ursa's only getting worse," Vicky answered. She sniffed and wiped her eyes. "It's okay, though. I'm sure she'll get better." Vicky walked over to the kitchen and handed Meemee the recipe. Maura watched her do this. She didn't like that Vicky was hiding how she truly felt. She walked down the Circle Stone Group's hallway and peered into Ursa and Vicky's room. Ursa was shaking in her bed. She turned around and walked towards Lenna's room.

"Lenna?" she said as she stepped in the doorway. She found the girl asleep and covered with blank sheets of paper. She stepped over to her and touched her shoulder. "Lenna, don't go to sleep yet, we're going to eat soon. Come eat." Lenna opened her eyes a little, grimaced at Maura, and then rolled over and went back to sleep. "Fine, starve," Maura said, and she walked out.

Lenna sat up in bed. She was pulled out of sleep by a bad dream. In the dream, she saw Ruller plunging into the volcano. Ursa followed him, and then she followed after Ursa. It all seemed so real. She looked around for someone to help her. She was worried.

"Lenna?" Ellia asked, walking into her room holding a torch. The light was blinding for a moment. "Are you okay? You were yelling." Lenna stared blankly at Ellia. She held her hands in front of her face and noticed that she was still in her clothes from ealier that day. She looked back at Ellia.

"Was I asleep?" Lenna asked. Ellia nodded. "I just had the strangest dream. Ruller fell into the volcano, and then Ursa, and then me."

"Ursa I can understand, but you? That doesn't make much sense. You're probably just worried." Ellia stared at her.

"I think that it was more than a dream, though. I think that it was trying to tell me that I had to follow Ruller."

"So you have to jump into the volcano?"

"I think that I need to go to the Dark Lands. Think of all the signs. Vicky finds that book in her room and it talks about Chaily and the Dark Lands, and now this dream."

"How are you going to get there, though?" Ellia asked. "You can't die."

"I hope that I don't have to," Lenna answered. They sat in silence for a minute.

"Do you think that Maia could bring you there?" Ellia finally asked.

"I didn't think of her. Let's find out!" Lenna said, standing up and walking into the hallway.

"Wait!" Ellia whispered loudly. "It's the middle of the night! She's sleeping!" Lenna continued to walk toward the Changing Group's hallway. Ellia quickly followed.

"Good, it brings me joy to annoy her," Lenna said. She stepped into the hall and walked to the second room on the left. Maia was buried under her blankets. Her head poked out, and her two ponytails draped over the side of the bed. Lenna put her hand on the girl's shoulder and shook her. "Maia, wake up."

"What is it?" Maia whispered, her voice cracking from sleep.

"Can you open portals to places that aren't on Laven?" Lenna asked.

"As in other planets?" Maia asked. "Probably. Good night."

"I mean as in the Dark Lands," Lenna said. Maia glared at her.

"The Dark Lands?" Maia asked, sitting up. "I have no idea. We don't even know if the Dark Lands exist."

"Well we need to find out," Lenna said. "Get up and try." Maia stood up, her long nightgown trailing behind her.

"Where did you get that?" Ellia asked. "You didn't have any clothes when you came here."

"Shenny made it for me when she was here," Maia answered. "You know, before you both messed up and let her leave." Lenna jerked forward, but Ellia quickly grabbed the end of her hair and pulled her back. Maia smiled. She reached out and tore open a portal in front of her. She dipped her hands inside and began to move the portal around. Lenna and Ellia watched over her shoulder. It looked like green water swirling in front of them, which was different from the way it had been the last time Maia opened a portal for them. "Okay," Maia said, "either you'll end up in the Dark Lands or empty space. Keep one hand holding onto Ellia's so that she can make sure that you're safe." She stepped back into her bed.

"Wish me luck," Lenna said, grabbing Ellia's hand and stepping into the portal. She was sucked in. Ellia's grasp released and she fell down into the darkness.

Chapter 8:
Paradise and Punishment

Lenna fell. She twisted and tumbled and flipped and fell. There was nothing around her. She could feel the difference between the air here and the air on Sio. There was no air here. She couldn't breathe. She was tumbling, and she could feel herself growing faint. In the distance there was a small light. She had to get to that light. Suddenly, she remembered what Divy had said to her: there's water in every living thing. That must include her. She put her hand on her stomach and drew out some water, bringing it to her mouth and forming a bubble, allowing her to breathe for now.

"This must be empty space," she thought to herself. "I might be able to move this." She swung her arms, but nothing happened. She clicked her heels together and a small jet of flames pushed her towards the light. She knew this was a risky move, considering she needed air to bring forth flames, but she had no other choice. Her bubble was decreasing in size, and soon she wouldn't be able to breathe again. She was nearing the light. Her flames began to flicker, and she once again began to fall.

She looked down at the light. She was above it when she began to fall. Before her were two large walls standing next to each other. Beside them was a small pond and sitting at the edge of the pond was a boy. He had curly, black hair, pale skin, and was hunched over with his hands on his knees. He wore a long, black cloak over his clothing.

The bubble around Lenna's mouth popped. She shouted for help. The boy looked up at her. He was expressionless, his eyes surrounded by dark bags. He stood up and pointed at her. Visible white air blew from his finger and caught her as she fell. She inhaled the air in and slowly hovered to the ground. She stared at the boy. They stood in silence for a moment and then ran into each others arms. Tears were falling from Lenna's eyes.

"How are you here? Why? How did you die?" she cried. "Chaily, what happened?"

"It's okay," Chaily said to her, holding her head against his chest. Lenna couldn't find his heartbeat. "I'll explain everything to you. It's okay."

"Why did you die?" she asked, sniffing and sitting down.

"I had no choice," Chaily answered, sitting next to her. "My job as a warrior is to guard the Death Doors." He pointed to the two walls behind them. Lenna stared up at them. The walls towered over them, and she noticed a vertical keyhole in the one on the left and a horizontal keyhole in the one on the right. Thin lines extended out from the keyholes towards the edges of the Doors. "The Doors are the entrances to the afterlife. The one on the left is paradise for those who led a good life. The one on the right is punishment for those who led an evil life. It's my job to determine who is allowed into which Door."

"So this is the Dark Lands after all?" Lenna asked. "Why you, though?"

"This is part of them," he said. "And this is my job. The warrior before me carried out this position as well after he died. He had disappeared at some point, and when I arrived this place was in chaos." Suddenly the area was illuminated in a bright flash of light, which immediately died down. "Hold on. Someone just died." He closed his eyes and took a breath. Lenna stared at him. Chaily's body fell backwards, and Lenna watched as a transparent version of him rushed out of his chest. Lenna sat and waited for a moment and then saw him fly back up. He reentered his body and sat up next to her. "Sorry," he said.

"What happened to you?" Lenna asked. She didn't know what was wrong with her. She was oddly quiet. She thought that she should be more frantic, or maybe happy, but instead she was calm.

"I can't collect souls when I'm in my body," Chaily answered. "My spirit is the only thing that can touch other spirits." He withdrew from his cloak a long sword. It was the weapon given to him by the previous Circle Stone Warriors. He dipped it into the pond sitting before them. A series of pictures flashed in the water, and then he withdrew his weapon. He turned to the Door on the left and inserted the sword into the vertical hole. Orange light traveled from the hilt into the hole and illuminated the lines leading out to the sides. "The man who died led a good life; he was kind. That's what the pond showed me. That's why I allowed him into paradise."

"Where did you go to get him, though?"

"Some people are better about dying than others are. The ones who accept death appear right here in front of me and are judged; the ones who have an attachment to something on Laven spend their time walking aimlessly in nothingness. They just walk. They never see another person or try to talk to one another. It's not until they surrender to the fact that they are dead that they are allowed to go further. That's when that light appears."

"You said that he just died, though." Lenna was completely emotionless.

"He died, saw where he was, thought, and accepted it. Then it was up to me to find him."

"That was fast." There was silence between them.

"Stop thinking that you're dead," Chaily said. He stared at her.

"What are you talking about?" Lenna asked.

"You're losing your emotions. You feel tired and confused, but you have no idea why it's not showing? You're in the place where only death exists, and therefore you feel dead. Don't feel dead. You'll turn into me."

"What do you mean?"

"Expressionless. You'll have no emotions. It's like this: I'm so excited to see you and know that you're not actually dead, and yet I haven't smiled once."

"How do you know that I'm not dead?" Lenna asked.

"I watched you come here."

"How?"

"I watched you in the pond. This place is great, really. I can do whatever I want. If I want this entire place to be filled with food, I can make that happen, eat, and never gain a single pound.

That's what's bad about being dead, though. You're never hungry. Smile." Lenna stared at him for a moment and then smiled.

"It just hit me that I'm here with you. Dead or alive, I'm happy that you're here," she said. "Now you have to smile for me."

"I can't."

"Dead people can't smile? Smile for me, please." She stood up over him and stared directly into his eyes. They were tired and cold and his expression never changed.

"It's not possible," he said. "I'm sorry." Lenna sat back down next to him.

"Explain to me what this pond is," she said.

"It lets me see people's lives as well as things going on on the planets. There are other planets out there, and all the people who die from them end up here as well. Let's see what's going on with our friends." He dipped his finger into the pool and the Circle Stone Room immediately appeared. Vicky, Grev, Vesa, and Lisha were sitting on the couches talking to each other. They were still wearing their sleeping clothes. Yawning, Rui entered the room and joined them.

"It looks like everyone's just waking up," Lenna said. "That's Vesa, Lisha, and Rui." When she mentioned Rui, she accidentally touched her finger to the water directly where his shoulder was. The boy jumped back as if someone had touched him. "What was that?"

"You touched him," Chaily answered. "The pond lets me, or I guess anyone, control what goes on on the planets. Want to do something kind for someone?" Lenna nodded. Chaily extended his hand over the water and slowly placed it down. The scene changed to a young girl sitting on the side of her house. "The wall is about to fall and kill her. At least, that's what's supposed to happen." He put his finger up against the wall. They waited a few seconds and the entire wall came crumbling down except for the part that she sat against. The girl screamed in shock, but then calmed down when she realized her good fortune. This was the part that Chaily was holding up. "The only difficult thing about saving that girl's life is that when one person doesn't die, another must." An old woman suddenly appeared in front of them.

"Finally," she said. "Thank you. It's about time." She smiled at the kids and waved at them. Chaily dipped his sword into the water, judged her, and opened the Door to paradise. She waved at them. "You two have fun now. You're both very lucky to have each other. Friendship is one of the most important things you can have. Always look out for each other."

"We will," Lenna said, quietly. The woman hobbled towards the open Door, which was letting a bright light shine into the area. She disappeared and the Door closed.

"So we just saved a small girl and put an old woman out of her misery. I think that's a pretty good deed, don't you?" Chaily asked. He sat back down next to Lenna.

"How do you pick who dies instead of the person who was supposed to?" she asked.

"It's random. It's always someone extremely old or sick. Someone who needs to die in order to be happy," he explained. "But enough with the questions, let's talk about why you're here. I'm surprised that Maia was so willing to do this for you, but then again, she'd do anything to get you out of the way."

"You saw the whole thing?"

"Most of it. I watch you all whenever I have spare time, but I also have to watch the rest of the universe. Spare time is rare. I wish I could've seen that dream you had. It sounded like a prediction."

"It's weird, that's not the first time that's happened to me. When I first arrived at Ixie, I was asleep. Right before I woke up, I had another one of those lucid dreams. I saw two lights above Sio, and then Gabent appeared on a mountaintop. Right after that, everything went dark, and I saw Ruller standing all alone, but he was dressed in a heavy cloak. It was strange."

"It's the Day of Two Suns," Chaily said. "No one can predict when it happens, but it's a day that lasts for the length of a week. Laven will rotate into another solar system and catch the light of a second sun. Two suns light the sky and the five islands are pulled together into one giant continent."

"How do the island move together?" Lenna asked.

"They're always moving, just like how our planet always moves around our sun. The movement of the islands is timed perfectly with the Day of Two Suns."

"How do you know about this two sun day?" Lenna asked.

"The pond," Chaily answered. "It lets me look forward to major events so that I can estimate how many deaths I'll have to deal with that day. I don't know who will die on those days, though." Lenna had to think for a minute in order to understand this.

"If the islands are together, Gabent could take control of them all at once!"

"That could be what he's hoping for," Chaily said. "What about the rest of that dream? What about Ruller? He's dead now. I hated seeing him appear before me. We talked for a little bit, and then he had to go into his Door. He was very good about it. Then Gabent showed up."

"Gabent knows about this place?" Lenna asked, shocked.

"He comes here to retrieve his spirits. He goes to the ones who are wandering around and takes them back down to Sio. Sometimes he even gets some from behind the Doors. I can't understand how he does it. It's strange that he has so many, though. He doesn't come here often. He must be getting them from somewhere else as well."

"But they're just dead people taken from here?"

"As far as I know. Come look." Chaily stood up and took her hand. He opened his other palm and a small light appeared and floated above it. Lenna stood up and followed as he walked far into the darkness, the light in his hand being their only guide. Then he stopped. They were standing on the edge of a cliff. Lenna looked down. Thousands of small, silver lights were moving far below them. "All of those lights are spirits. They can't see each other, but we can see them. Gabent just goes down there and takes as many as he needs. Since I arrived, though, he's been having difficulty taking them. As soon as I see him, he's pretty easy to expel."

"Why don't you just kill him?"

"His spirit comes here, not his body," Chaily answered. "I tried to capture him, but he escaped each time."

They walked back to the Death Doors. They sat back down, and Lenna, resting her head on Chaily's shoulder, looked down at the scene in the pond. It had changed back to their friends, and by now everyone was awake.

"I can read what's in that book," Chaily said, looking towards Vicky.

"How?" Lenna asked sleepily.

"You need to wake up," he said. "When I first saw what it was I summoned an index that showed me what each symbol meant. Ruller also explained to me what the spell he cast on Vicky was." Lenna sat up, confused.

"Vicky didn't tell us that he cast something on her. What was it?" Lenna asked. Chaily looked into the pond.

"Watch this," he said, "it looks like you're about to find out. This is the first time that Vicky has actually dealt with the book since she received it, besides that time with you." Lenna looked in. Vicky was holding the book open and staring at it with Sensho and Kit. They had decoded as many of the symbols as they could.

"Okay," Vicky said, "I'm positive that this is the summoning spell." She pointed at the first page.

"You're sure?" Sensho confirmed. "I want to make sure that we made no mistakes in solving this."

"Positive," Vicky answered. "It's the page that Ruller read from the night that we met. He showed it to me and then cast the spell on Ursa. It was funny."

"What did he summon?" Kit slowly asked.

"Her gloves," she answered. "He just stuck out his hand and said, *'Coget!'*." A pair of gloves flew into the room and hit Vicky in the face. She stared at them for a moment. There were yellow gems on the back of them. Everyone in the Circle Stone Room was silent. They were all staring at the gloves.

"He gave her his magic?!" Lenna shouted in surprise.

"Correct." Chaily answered. "The transfer spell appeared in his book just before he died. It was his last resort." They stared into the pond and watched Vicky. She was trying out as many of Ruller's spells that she could remember. They watched as she tossed fire with Lisha, sent objects flying to Rui, and teleported in a stylish fashion from place to place.

"It's funny," Lenna noted, "Vicky's much more fun about her spells than Ruller was. I mean, just look at how she teleports." It was true, every time Vicky teleported something different happened. The first time was the way Ruller did it. A green ball of light surrounded her and made her disappear, and then the light reappeared in a different location, making her reappear. The second time, however, she spun around and the light spun around her as well until it formed a ball to make her disappear. The third time, she clapped her hands. A ring of green light shot out from the center of her body, and then expanded into the ball. "I think that Vicky's going to be much more imaginative about the way the magic is used than Ruller was. I guess something good came out of all of this, right?"

"I guess so," Chaily answered. At that moment two men appeared in front of them. One was wearing black and red armor and the other was wearing blue and silver armor. The one in black and red had a knife in his back, and the one in blue and silver had a knife in his stomach. "You killed each other?"

"Our villages are at war," the man in blue and silver stated.

Chaily dipped his sword into the pond. Faster than before, the scenes from the men's lives flashed in the water. Chaily stood up when they ended. He inserted his sword into the vertical keyhole and waited for the Door to open. The bright light blinded Lenna once again. "For living a good life," he said to the man in red and black, "you're rewarded." The man walked into the light and disappeared. "And for living an evil life," Chaily said, opening the Punishment Door, "you will suffer." When the Door opened, no light fell out. The man walked through the doorway, and the moment his body was entirely inside, he disappeared and a ring of fire shot out. The Punishment Door slammed shut while the Paradise Door slowly closed.

"I thought it would be the other way around," Lenna said. "I thought the man in black and red would be the evil one."

"Things aren't always as they seem," Chaily said. "Just because someone looks bad on the outside does not mean that they are bad on the inside. It's the same thing with strength. If one looks weak on the outside, they might actually be one of the strongest people that a person will ever know." Lenna thought for a moment of Divy, the skinny boy who was able to take down two people at once.

"They gave me an idea," Lenna said. "Maybe we've been approaching this situation incorrectly. Every time we try to destroy Gabent, we wait for him to come to us or we attack from a distance. Maybe we need to go straight to the source this time."

"Remember," Chaily said, "their plans ended in their own deaths."

"Yes, but ours won't, I'm sure of it," Lenna said. "How do I get back home?" Chaily pointed to the pond. The scene of their friends had reappeared once again.

"Jump in." Lenna stared at the water for a second, and then looked at her friend.

"I don't want to leave yet," she said.

"You don't have a choice," Chaily said. "Stay here too long and you might not be able to leave. Go." He stood and helped her up. She leaned into his arms and pressed her head against his chest. Chaily's lips lightly touched the top of her head, and then he straightened up. "You have to do what you have to do." Lenna released him and turned towards the water.

"Are you sure it's time for me to go?" she asked, turning.

"Positive," he answered. He gave her a light push and she jumped down. She didn't get wet, nor splash any of the water over the edge. She simply fell and soon found herself standing between Kit and Maura, who jumped at her sudden appearance. Her emotions came flooding back into her body.

"Lenna!" Vicky shouted. "Guess what?"

"I already know! I saw it all from the Dark Lands!" She walked over and hugged Vicky.

"Did you find out what you needed to?" Ellia asked.

"Yes I did. I found Chaily, too." Everyone stared at her, waiting for her to explain. "He's fine. He's guarding the Dark Lands. He judges the people who die and makes sure that they are either rewarded for living a good life or punished for living a bad life. And guess what?" she said, turning to Divy, who raised his eyebrow at her. "The spirits that Gabent uses *are* actually dead people!"

"Yeah?" Divy asked.

"Yeah! Gabent goes to the Dark Lands and takes spirits from there. Then they follow his orders. Chaily tries to keep them all safe, though."

"So we could be fighting people that we know that have died?" Mira asked.

"I didn't think of it that way," Lenna said.

"I'm sure he isn't with Gabent," Kita quietly whispered to Mira. No one heard her.

"Why were we able to see one of the spirits when we froze him?" Divy asked.

"I—I don't know," Lenna stammered. She was beginning to become flustered.

"That's okay," Ellia said. "What else did you find out?"

"Well, Chaily has this pond that lets him see what goes on here. That's how I found out that Vicky has Ruller's powers. I also have an idea of what we can do. I think that we need to go into Gabent's castle."

"All of us?" Lisha asked nervously.

"Maybe not all of us," Lenna said, "but definitely some of us. I think that this time, instead of trying to play it safe, we should try attacking head on."

"And if we mess up?" Divy asked.

"Then Maia or Vicky will get us out of there." She stared at everyone in the room. They all had skeptical looks on their faces, and she knew that she wasn't doing a good job of convincing them. "Let's just try it."

"Lenna," Sensho said, "I think that you're taking your resources for granted. This is a very dangerous idea that you have. You know that Gabent will not hold back if you are found. Plus, he may still not know that we are alive, let alone that there are more of us now."

"Yes, but if we really think this through, we'll be able to come up with a plan that even Gabent won't expect!"

"You do not know anything about the castle, though. For one thing, where are you expecting to find Gabent?" Lenna thought for a moment.

"Maia can find that out!" she said, running over to her.

"Excuse me?" Maia asked. "I didn't volunteer for this job."

"For once I have to agree with Maia," Maura said. "We can't send her in there alone."

"But she's perfect for this job!" Lenna said. "Please!"

"No," Maura said, "she doesn't have to go. I'll go, I like a challenge."

"How do you expect to blend in?" Lenna asked. Maura stood up.

"I'm a shape shifter, remember?" She smiled at Lenna and disappeared. "I'll go into the castle and meet whoever you send in later. I'll figure out how everything works and what we can all expect." She reappeared in the same spot. Lenna turned to Sensho for permission.

"If you go in there," he said to Maura, "you have no idea how careful you must be. You have never faced Gabent before. In fact, you have never even faced a spirit before. If you go in there, I do not care what you find, you never make yourself visible, do you understand me?"

"Yes," Maura said.

"The only reason that I will allow this is because I trust you," he turned to Lenna, "and not because I expect it to work, but because I believe that we may be able to find out information that we did not know before. Maia, you will bring Maura to the castle. I want you to go into the castle with her so you see where you send her. When Lenna decides who will go in later, you will all meet there." Maia stared angrily at Sensho for a moment, and then nodded her head. She stood up, spun around, and disappeared. Then a portal appeared.

"Get in," came Maia's voice. Maura disappeared as well. Everyone stared at the portal for a moment, and then it snapped shut. A few seconds later it reappeared again. Maia stepped out. "I know where I'm sending them."

"Good," Sensho said. "Lenna, figure out what you are going to do with this before I change my mind."

"Can I see all of the leaders again?" Lenna asked. Meemee, Divy, Ellia, Rui, and Vesa stood up and walked over to the planning area. "Maia, since Kit can't speak that well yet, you're the leader of the Changing Group." Maia walked over to the other leaders. Lenna quickly joined them.

"Okay, what do you all think we should do?" Ellia asked, taking control.

"I'm still not very comfortable with this . . ." Meemee said.

"Really, it will be okay!" Lenna responded. "I have faith in everyone in here! We can all communicate with each other; we'll help people who need help!"

"Fine, but I think that we should only send in a few people. One person from each group," Meemee said.

"Well if we're doing that, we might as well just go," Vesa said. "I mean all of the leaders."

"That actually might be a good idea," Divy said. "We have a good collection of powers with all of us here."

"That's right," Ellia said. "Lenna, this is your plan, you're going to need to conduct it. I'll stay back and you can go into the castle."

"Maura's already in the castle," Maia said. "Kit and I will stay behind."

"Now is that a good idea?" Divy asked the group. "Do you think that Maia or Vicky should come with us in case we need to get out quickly?"

"Vicky will be in danger," Rui added.

"Maia," Meemee said, "are you willing to go into the castle with us?"

"I'll do whatever I have to," Maia said. "I've realized at this point that I have no choice."

"I think that both Maia and Vicky should stay behind," Vesa said. "Maia's going to be the most accurate about transporting people into the castle if we need them. Vicky's still learning."

"But she's learning fast," Lenna said.

"Maybe not fast enough to know exactly where we are. Maia can locate us if we contact her."

"And we have Maura on the inside already," Meemee said. "Where are your gems?"

"On my headband," Maia answered, twisting it on her head. Two small pink gems were revealed.

"Let me try something," Meemee said. To Maia's disliking she grabbed the headband off of her head and touched the gems to her bracelet. Instantly the gems already on the bracelet disappeared, and a pink gem, a crimson gem, and a purple gem appeared. "Great! Now I can communicate with you three as well. Can I have everyone else's gems?" Meemee quickly added the gems for the other groups to her collection and handed them back to the respective warriors.

"So it's me, Lenna, Rui, Vesa, Maura, and Meemee going in?" Divy asked.

"Correct," Vesa said.

"What should everyone staying behind do?" Maia asked.

"Stay in here and wait until we need help," Meemee answered. "You can decide if there's anything special that they should do."

"I'll go tell them that," Lenna said. She walked over to the rest of the warriors, who were relaxing and waiting to find out what they should do. "Ellia and Maia are going to be in charge of all of you. We're going into the castle and we'll let you know what you should do when the time comes." Everyone in the room nodded.

"Let's go," Maia said, calling Lenna over and rubbing one of the gems on her headband. After whispering into it, she put the headband back on her head. "Maura knows that you all are coming. She'll be in the room that I send you all to. She says to get behind the curtains." Maia opened the portal and allowed everyone going to the castle to step inside.

Chaily watched this entire plan unfold. He stared down at the pond, wondering what would happen next. As he changed the picture to the room that they were traveling to, he noticed two spirits walking in. He quickly pressed his fingers on both of them and sent them to another part of the castle. Instantly, the souls of four people appeared before him. He sighed at the deed he had done.

Chapter 9:
Murders and Secrets

Vesa fell out of the portal and into the room first. Next was Rui, then Meemee, Divy, and finally, Lenna. They all looked around for a moment and then ducked behind the curtains, just as Maura had told them to. They waited in silence, and then the door to the room opened.

"Okay, good," came a whisper.

"Maura?" Divy asked.

"Yes," Maura answered. "I've figured out everything that I can. This place is crawling with spirits, so we need to be really careful. Once we leave this room there's a long hallway that leads to a circular room. In that room there are eight doors and no way of opening them. There wasn't even a crack for me to slip through. I guess that Lenna can help open them, and from there I think that we should split up."

"Split up?" Vesa whispered. "We don't know this place and none of us can be invisible."

"How about we see what's behind those doors before we split up," Meemee suggested.

"Okay, fine, let's go," Maura said.

"Where are you?" Rui asked.

"Oh, right," Maura said. After a moment, a large cloak appeared in the room and hovered above the floor.

"You turned into a spirit?" Lenna asked.

"It's the easiest way for me to get around," Maura answered. She led them out the door and told them to wait so that she could check for any spirits. She glided down the hallway and opened the door at the other end. After a moment, the sleeve of her cloak lifted, and her invisible arm gestured for them to follow. They stepped into the circular room and found themselves staring at eight stone doors.

"Oh, this will be easy," Lenna whispered. She stretched her arms out to the side, opened her hands, and fell to the floor, smacking it hard. Eight booms were heard as the doors crumbled.

"You want to be a little louder?!" Maura shouted at her. A swarm of spirits appeared in one of the rooms revealed, and they were gliding towards them quickly. "Split up!" Maura shouted.

"I don't think that's the best idea!" Divy argued, but as he was saying that, Vesa yelped and sprinted into one of the rooms. "Everyone stay together! We're stronger this way!" Before he could convince them, though, Rui had flown into another room, and Maura, now in her regular form, had run into another. "Lenna! Meemee!" The two girls had already gone their separate ways before Divy shouted their names. Desperate, he ran into one of the two rooms that none of his friends had gone into. As the spirits flooded into the circular room, eight new doors appeared. Although this seemed like an obstacle, the spirits had the freedom to open whichever one they chose.

*   *   *

Maura looked behind her as she ran. She saw Divy standing alone in the circular room, but then he ran off to the side. A new stone door appeared behind her, shutting her in, and she turned back around to see a long hallway before her. It was strangely familiar to her, but she couldn't place where she had seen it. She looked back over her shoulder. The door was the same distance away as it was before. She hadn't moved from this spot, even though she was running. She stopped and walked back to the door. Above it was a small picture of a head with light coming out of the forehead.

She looked down at her feet. Dark blue clouds had begun to drift into the room. She stepped back and watched the walls disappear. Maura frantically looked around for some kind of help, but all she could see was sky. A loud cackle filled the room, and two people began to fly around her.

"Bria?" she asked. She recognized the cackle as that of her sister. She stared at the people flying around her. One was completely white and the other was completely black. They stopped and stared at her. They were naked, genderless bodies, and she had seen them before on Helite. She knew now where she was. This was no longer a room in Gabent's castle, but a nightmare which she had been repeatedly dreaming for years. Out of the clouds grew three long, bent spikes. They rose up on top of a long staff. There was a large, square hole in the staff, which now towered over her.

"No," she said, turning to the black and white people. "No, please! I know what you're going to do. Please, don't!" They rushed at her and pushed her up into the air, placing her in the square hole and flying around it. Maura could feel the room becoming warmer.

"Please! Stop this!" she pleaded, her eyes beginning to water. She knew what was coming to her. The hole was suddenly filled with flames, and Maura screamed in pain as the fire from her dream began to scorch her body. The people stopped circling the staff and perched on it, one on each side. They stared at the tortured girl, and then filled the room with a bright white light.

*   *   *

Rui beat his wings fiercely. He heard the new door slam behind him, and he stopped midair in the room he was now in. It was square and completely made of stone. Above the door was a small picture of a torso with light coming from its center.

Rui looked down at his staff. He flew over to one of the walls and touched the tip of the ruby to it. It began to glow, taking in the energy from the stone. He removed it and pointed it at the wall again. A dark brown beam shot out, exploding a hole in the wall for him to escape from.

The moment the wall opened, however, purple gas began to creep into the room. Rui didn't dare go near it, and so he flew to the other side of the room. The gas continued to fill up the room, and it was beginning to close in on him. He began to swing his staff in an attempt to send it away, but it only continued to come closer. It was up to his neck now, sending chills through his entire body. When it reached his mouth, he had no choice but to breathe it in.

As the gas entered him his throat completely dried. He could feel it closing, and he slowly hovered to the ground. He fell to his knees and began to choke, his lungs burning

Chaily watched this happen from the pond in the Dark Lands. "They can't lose someone this quickly," he said, staring at Rui. "He isn't going to die, not already." He bent over the pond and blew directly on Rui. The winged boy could feel Chaily's breath blowing on him, although he had no idea where it was coming from. The gas parted and slowly thinned out, leaving Rui lying on the floor, weak. Chaily looked up, waiting for the soul of Rui's replacement to appear. Right on cue, a twelve year old girl appeared before him. She had short black hair and familiar clothes. Chaily stared at her hands and examined her gloves. Six yellow gems lit up the fabric.

"Hi!" Ursa said happily.

"You realize where you are, right?" Chaily asked.

"I think I figured it out."

"Does anyone know?"

"Not yet, I was alone. They will soon though, I'm sure. I'm so happy that I'm not sick anymore. Is there any way I can say good-bye to Vicky?"

"No, I'm sorry."

*   *   *

Lenna heard the door slam behind her as she entered into a square room with an extremely high ceiling. There was a large, circular, and ornate window at the top of the wall to her right; however, it wasn't letting much light into the room. The entire area was very dim. Lenna rested against one of the walls for a few minutes.

Right after she caught her breath, the door slid open. About fifty spirits came rushing in, the sleeves of their cloaks extended towards her. She lifted the bottom of her skirt and jumped up, pushing against the wall with her foot. She moved the air under her so that it propelled her to the next wall, from which she pushed off again and continued upwards. As she flew, she watched the spirits' hoods turn up towards her.

Suddenly, one of the spirits jumped into the air and flew towards her. The rest quickly followed, sleeves outstretched. She released her skirt and pushed her hand towards the leading one. It fell backwards as she froze the inside of the cloak, shattering upon hitting the ground. As it fell, it obstructed five others, all of which fell as well. The rest simply flew around them and continued towards her. Keeping her eyes on her enemies, Lenna didn't remember to watch her footing on the wall, and as she pressed with her foot she slid a few feet downwards before making a weak push off. An invisible hand from one of the spirits grabbed her skirt and tried to pull her down. She quickly froze it, and the face and body of a young woman fell to the ground.

The next time she pushed off the wall she spun in the air, twirling two streams of water in her hands. She looked below her at the oncoming danger and shot the streams down. They cut their way through the spirits, making two holes in the mob flying towards her. She turned her head towards the wall she was soaring to and reached out. When her hand touched it, she pressed finger holes into it. Lenna hung there for a moment and then touched her other hand to the wall, pulling out a flat ledge for her to perch upon. She stood on it and swung her arm through the air in front of her. Immediately the water in the air froze, making a heavy sheet of ice which she dropped on the spirits. One by one they were pushed down and crushed.

Lenna looked at the wall opposite her. The window was facing her and was just a few feet above where she was now. She saw it as her only way out, and so she jumped up, kicked out a few strong bursts of air, and watched the glass come closer and closer.

*   *   *

Meemee clutched her belt as she ran. She wanted to be sure that she had a bomb in hand in case anything tried to catch her by surprise. She stopped in the middle of the room she was now in. One half of it was lit by a small window in the ceiling, and the other half was barely touched by the light. The door slammed behind her, and she stared at it. There was a picture of a shattered bone above it. Turning and squinting, she was able to make out a dark figure sitting against one of the walls. The figure slowly stood up and stepped forward.

"It's about time you showed up," said a familiar voice. Meemee was silent for a moment.

"Shenny?" she asked. The hooded girl stepped forward into the light. Meemee stared at her. The once prim and neat girl was now unbecoming and unsmiling. She had a layer of dirt on her face and hands, and her dress and apron were torn in various places. When she pulled her hood down, Meeemee found that her hair was unkempt and her face had thinned out. Her dress and apron had become darker. They were usually pink and white, but they were now grey. "What's happened to you?"

"I've spent all my time in here, that's what's happened," Shenny answered. "As soon as I left I figured out how to sneak into the castle and I've been hiding in the shadows ever since. I arrived in this room just a little while before you did. I've been trying to figure out its purpose."

"But you seem so different," Meemee said. "It hasn't been that long."

"Yes, but it seems that I've adjusted to these conditions rather quickly," Shenny said. "Apparently I haven't been pulling my weight when it comes to saving Sio, so here I am. I've been able to survive, what? Three, four days under Gabent's nose? It's surprising how much can happen in that time."

"I can see that you're still angry."

"Still angry?" Shenny laughed. "That doesn't even begin to explain it. If that is what one person thinks of me, what does everybody else think? You all keep that hidden and then talk behind my back? Did you think that's what I would want? Did you all think that you were being nice to me?" She stepped forward and disappeared into the ground. Meemee ran over to the spot where Shenny was. A large hole had appeared and the girl had fallen right into it. "This was not here before!" she exclaimed.

"Here, grab my hand, I'll pull you out," Meemee said, reaching inside. The moment she reached in, however, metal bars shot out of the sides of the hole, blocking her hand. Shenny reached up and tapped the bars.

"This will be easy," she said, pulling a knife from inside her sleeve. Meemee saw the faint glisten of three pink gems on it. It was the knife that Sio had given her before they faced Gabent for the very first time. Shenny swung her arm up, knife in hand, and sliced through the edge of the bars. She did this again on the opposite side of the bars, and they fell with a loud clang.

"Take my hand," Meemee said again.

"I don't need your help," Shenny protested. She flung her arms up, throwing two chains out from inside her sleeves. They shot past Meemee's head and pierced the ceiling. Shenny quickly climbed out and pulled her chains back to her. "There are spears in the tips."

"When did you get them?" Meemee asked.

"I had Lenna make them for me when no one was watching," Shenny answered. "You'd be surprised what else I have. And now I'm going to leave you once again. Bye." She ran to one of the walls in the light and jumped up, pushing off of it from a higher point with her foot and throwing one of her chains through the window. She climbed up and out of the room.

"Wait!" Meemee shouted after her. "What about me?" There was no answer. She sat down against one of the walls and waited for something to happen. Perhaps someone would open the door, or maybe Shenny would come back for her. She even wouldn't have minded if the spirits came after her. At least then she might have a chance to go somewhere else. She stood up and walked to the dark side of the room in hopes that there was something hidden which she couldn't see. After running her hand over the wall, however, she found that there was nothing there but stone.

Meemee walked back into the center of the room and began to pace.

"Hello? Can anybody hear me?" she shouted. At that moment, the entire room began to tremble. Meemee looked around and saw that the two walls to her sides were moving closer to her.

"Hello?!" she shouted frantically. "Somebody help me!" She began to run around, trying to find some way for her to escape. She looked up at the window that Shenny had crawled out from. One of the walls was beginning to cover it, and it was soon completely covered, leaving Meemee in the dark.

She took one of the bombs from her belt and threw it into the darkness. The room was illuminated for a moment as the bomb exploded, showing the walls just a few feet from her. If she didn't act fast, she would be crushed. She withdrew another bomb and threw it in the same direction as the previous one. This time, a small hole appeared in the light. It was the hole that the previous bomb had blasted. Meemee ran forward and put her hands on the wall where the hole was. It was one of the moving walls, and she was now stepping backwards as she tried to locate her only means of survival. At the last second, she found the opening and quickly climbed inside. There was a loud boom as the walls collided.

Hunched in the shape of a ball, Meemee stretched her hand out a few inches. She could feel the other wall next to her. She bent her arm in an uncomfortable position and put her hand on her bracelet. She couldn't see what color the gems were, so she had no idea whom she would call, but she rubbed her finger across one of the gems anyway.

"Hello?" she asked. "Who am I calling right now?"

"Lisha," said the voice from her bracelet. "Why can't I see you?"

"It's all dark where I am," Meemee answered. "Lisha, I don't know what to do. I'm trapped in a hole that I made in a wall. I can't move. What should I do?"

"Um, I don't know," Lisha answered.

"Well can you let me talk to someone who does know?"

"Give me that," Meemee heard someone in the background say. "You're no help to her. Meemee, it's Mira, do you have enough room to explode your way out?"

"Not without hurting myself," Meemee answered.

"Do you have anything else there to help you?"

"No."

"Okay, maybe Maia . . ."

"Wait," Meemee said, "something's happening. The walls are opening again." Meemee tumbled to the floor, and before she could look around she was dragged away.

*   *   *

Divy slowly advanced through the room that he entered. It was large library with a window covering the entire far wall. Several tables and chairs were set up throughout the room. He walked over to the window and looked out. He was facing away from the mountains and could only see flat land. He tried to locate the entrance to the Circle Stone Room, but there was no landmark to indicate where it was. He was sure that he wouldn't be able to enter anyway, considering that he wasn't a Circle Stone Warrior.

Before he could step away from the window, the door to the room slammed open and countless spirits poured inside. Some flew in while others shot beams at him from behind the pack. Divy overturned one of the longer tables and ducked down behind it. A bright beam shot a hole straight through this defense just a few feet away from him. He jumped up and moved his arm in front of him. A large wall of ice appeared in front of him, and the beams being shot deflected off of it.

Divy stayed behind the wall and waited, hoping that the spirits would eventually tire themselves out. He soon realized that this idea, like the table, was a lost cause, because how could something that isn't alive tire itself out? His only option was to fight back. He stared through the ice at his enemies. They were beginning to come towards him. Scared, he ran out from behind his wall and jumped on one of the tables. One spirit flew towards him, and at the last moment he jumped out of the way, closing his fist and pulling away. A stream of clear, almost glowing water appeared from underneath the spirit's cloak, and soon the empty article of clothing fell to the floor. For some reason, Divy was delighted by this.

Divy began to twirl this stream around his head and shoot it at the spirits, using it like a whip. With each spirit it hit, the stream extended with the added water which it took from the cloak, and

110

the boy laughed happily as he did this. Divy soon had enough water at his disposal to release it as a large wave, and each spirit fell as it was hit and its invisible body was absorbed. Divy swept his arm through the air, bringing the water up, and held his hand behind his back, moving the now swirling ball of water behind him. He stood on the table, waiting to see what would happen next.

After a moment of silence, another surge of spirits came rushing in. The boy couldn't help himself but to burst out in laughter. He moved his hands around, bringing the water in front of him. He spun it around his body, making a protective twister of water. He grinned and continued to spin the water around him, and it was soon pulling the spirits' bodies in as well. Water flew from each cloak and was added to the twister as it spun more rapidly.

Divy kept this going and soon the entire room was filled with water. More spirits opened the door and were pushed back by the wave which came rushing out. Using this as an opportunity to escape, Divy broke the large window and jumped out.

"This is high!" he shouted as he fell. He swung his arm below him, making an ice slide appear. He slid down, adding to the slide as he went, and circled the castle several times. As he slid, he withdrew his necklace with his spare hand.

"Lisha!" he said quickly. "I need someone to open the door to the room!"

"Okay give us a minute," Lisha answered.

"Now!" he said, noticing that he was nearing the ground. He extended the slide in the general direction of the Circle Stone Room and noticed a small hole appear to his right. He moved his hand in a right curved direction, and the slide quickly adjusted to this command. He had picked up more speed than he liked, and he made a guess as to how to enter the hole in order to fall into the hallway and not into a wall. He extended his arm out, touching the slide to the edge of the entrance. He was a few feet away when he noticed that he had guessed incorrectly, and he quickly twisted his hand, turning the edge in the correct direction. He flew down into the hallway and landed at the feet of his friends. A shatter erupted through the air as his slide fell to the ground and broke.

$*$ $*$ $*$

Vesa ran into one of the rooms, looking over her shoulder the entire time. She sprinted down a long hallway with a dark purple carpet down the center and stopped to rest at the end, leaning up against a large, wooden door. Nervous, she slowly and quietly cracked the door open. She listened closely to hear if anyone was in the next room. There was silence, and so she stuck her head in. The room on the other side was extremely large. The dark purple carpet continued to run halfway through the room and then expanded, entirely covering the other half. Tall, arched windows lined two of the four marble walls; six on each side. Opposite her a large, black curtain draped from the ceiling to the carpet. Seeing that there was no one in the room, she stepped in.

The girl walked along the carpet, advancing to the other side of the room. The door closed by itself behind her, but she guessed it was built to do that. She made it to the point where the carpet began to expand before someone spoke.

"You should learn not to trust what you see," said a deep voice. Vesa began to quickly turn in all directions, looking for the source of the voice. The curtain in front of her opened up, revealing a tall man with a hard, pale face, and short, jet black hair. He was dressed entirely in black armor and he sat on a large throne. To his right was a young man with long brown hair, dark eyes, and light skin who was dressed entirely in brown armor of different shades. His belt was equipped with a sword, daggers, rope, and chains, and he was seated on a smaller throne. To the man's left was an ancient man hunched over on a large wooden throne. He was dressed completely in normal, casual clothing. Sitting on the floor next to the center throne was a young boy, roughly eight years old, with short black hair, dark eyes, and dark skin, who was dressed in a long, black robe with blue trim. Vesa's eyes widened at this sight, and she turned and tried to run away. Right as she stepped to move, however, a transparent, light blue ball appeared around her, holding her in her current position. The ball rose up and hovered a few inches off of the ground, holding Vesa in the air with it. The young boy with the dark skin pointed and the ball flew over to the four of them. "Excellent work, Tohphus," Gabent said.

"Thank you, sir; I've been practicing ever since the volcanoes erupted," Tohphus said. "Why did Purple think she could run away?"

"Because she's new and doesn't know who she's fighting against," Gabent answered. "Look at the fear in her eyes. Delightful, isn't it? Cabe, who is she?"

"I've never seen her before," said the old man. "But we know that the children have no problem adding members to their team."

"True," Gabent said. "Perhaps we should get rid of this one, then." He held his hand out to Tohphus. The boy giggled and moved his hand over Gabent's. As he did this the ball moved in front of Gabent and its color changed from light blue to dark purple. Gabent closed his hand into a tight fist. The ball slowly began to shrink. Vesa's body bent over, trying to fit into the increasingly small space that it had. Soon the girl was hunched over in an unnatural position, her bones at their breaking points.

Before Vesa's body could snap, a knife flew down from the ceiling and pierced Gabent's hand. The ball instantly burst and Vesa fell to the ground, her body twitching lightly. To the right of the thrones a young girl jumped to the ground from the ceiling.

"Shenny?" Vesa asked, holding herself up with her arm.

"This one I do know," Gabent said, standing up and extending his palm towards her. Just like Vesa, she was instantly trapped in a transparent, dark purple ball. To be safe he trapped Vesa as well and brought the two balls together, forming one.

"Oh, this one I know as well," said the young man in brown. He stood up and walked around the trapped warriors. "This is the one whose house I helped to destroy. This is also the one whose parents I killed when this all started."

"You killed her parents, Lenny?" Tohphus asked, frowning

"Yes, I did what needed to be done. I saw how she was helping the children, so I thought that she needed to be taught a lesson."

"And obviously that didn't work," Gabent remarked angrily. "You're too kind, Lenzar. It seems that she has only become stronger since then." He turned around and struck Lenzar in the face. Blood was smeared across his cheek, but it was blood from Gabent's hand. "Failure to deal with these annoyances will not be tolerated." There was a loud crash on the other side of the room. One of the windows shattered as a body burst through the glass. Lenna slid across the floor as she failed to make a sufficient landing, but she was on her feet in a split second.

"Gabent!" she shouted when she noticed him. She raised both of her hands in the air, took a deep breath, pulled them down to her ribs, and pushed forward, breathing out. Two pillars of fire shot from her palms, one hitting and breaking Vesa and Shenny's prison and the other just missing Gabent, but setting fire to the curtain behind him. Lenzar and Cabe stood up and stepped in front of Gabent, ready to defend him. However, before either of them could react, a dark red ball appeared around Lenna. "What is this?!" she shouted from inside.

"Think of it as a cage," Gabent answered. He turned and trapped Vesa in the same kind of ball and dragged the two together, forming one. "Where's the other one?"

"Right here," Shenny answered. Using Lenna and Vesa as a distraction, she had slipped behind Lenzar and pulled his arms behind his back. "I knew that you looked familiar," she said in his ear. "As they say, 'a life for a life'. Isn't it sad that you took *two* lives?" She brought forth her gemmed knife and dug it into Lenzar's back. Twisting it and pulling out, she let his body fall.

"Shenny . . ." Lenna said quietly, shocked. Vesa was speechless. Gabent quickly trapped Shenny and threw her with the other two.

"You didn't see her coming?" Cabe asked Tohphus, angrily.

"You didn't either," Tohphus answered, scowling from his spot on the floor.

"It doesn't matter," Gabent stated. "Cabe, stay alive. Back down." Cabe retreated through a door behind the burning curtain.

"Can I have Lenny's throne?" Tohphus asked.

"Fine," Gabent answered. Tohphus giggled happily and stood up. His robe was significantly oversized, his hands completely covered by the sleeves and the bottom trailing on the floor. He scampered over to Lenzar's throne and climbed up. The seat was far too high for him.

At that moment, the door to the room slammed open and three spirits walked in, dragging Meemee, Rui, and Maura behind them. All three were tied up and had different expressions on their faces. Rui looked as if he was about to be sick, Maura's eyes were wide open and she was shaking in fear, her skin bright pink and blistered, and Meemee was trying desperately to be freed from her bindings.

"Ah, this one," Gabent said, bending down to touch Maura's cheek. She winced in pain when he made contact. "She begged for her life. So weak." The three were released and thrown into the red prison with the others. Instantly, the ball sank into the floor and was sent to a dimly lit room in which it would stay.

"Water," Maura pleaded, turning to Lenna. "Please." Lenna pulled forth as much as she could and covered Maura with it.

"Shenny, what are you doing here?" Lenna asked.

"Fighting Gabent," Shenny answered. "I've been here ever since I left." She held up her knife and wiped the blood off with her apron. "Now don't you think we should be calling for help?" she asked. Everyone withdrew their gems and began to rub them at once.

"Is anyone else having problems with this?" Meemee asked.

"This shouldn't be happening," Vesa said. "The gems should work wherever we are."

"It's probably the spell," Shenny said. "We can't communicate with anyone."

"Great," Meemee said.

"Where is Divy?" Rui asked.

"Has anyone seen him?" Lenna asked. She was answered with blank stares. "Well hopefully he'll bring help if he got out of the castle. Maura, your headband is twisted. Here, I'll fix it. Are you okay? What happened to you?" Maura's eyes were tearing and she was still shaking. Her clothes were singed and torn in various places.

"The room that I went to," she explained, "brought my worst nightmare to life. I can't face what I saw."

"What happened?" Rui asked, trying to figure out a way to fit his staff comfortably in the small amount of space that they had.

"Did you ever wonder why I wear this headband, besides the fact that it holds my gems?" she asked. "On Helite, this type of headband is to be worn by princesses only. It turns out that Maia is actually my successor, but she'll never admit it. That's why there's so much tension between us."

"You're the princess of Helite?" Vesa asked.

"Yes," Maura answered. "Back when I was partially in power, I met a boy named Duner. Duner and I went on an adventure to find five dragons that were going to destroy the planet out of rage. Each dragon controlled a different element: air, earth, water, fire, and empty space. Duner had a weapon called the Elemental Rod. At the top of the Rod was a small square box with an opening in the center. It almost looked like a lantern. This rod was used to take power from the dragons, and it turns out that if you take power from the dragons, you receive what you took. By accident, I received the fire dragon's power.

"Now, we weren't the only ones chasing the dragons. My older sister, Bria, was looking to harness their powers as well. Bria had two followers, Clan and Roi. They were almost as wicked as Bria was. They would torture Duner and me to the point where we were begging for death, and then they would leave us there to suffer. Ever since I met them, I couldn't get them out of my head. This was two years ago, I was only fourteen." Maura thought of the younger warriors back in the Circle Stone Room. "Anyway," she continued, "my dream goes like this. Clan and Roi trap me in the box at the top of a giant version of Duner's staff. They circle me and torture me by setting my body on fire. This time was so much worse because it was real." A tear ran down her cheek, but Lenna wiped it away.

"What happened to your fire power?" she asked.

"I let Duner take it right before I came here. It was rightfully his, anyway. It's his family's legacy, not mine. I have my shape-shifting power now. I didn't know about it back when this all was happening."

"That's a really difficult experience, I'm sure," Meemee said. "I'm sorry that you've had such a short time to recover from it, and who knows how much of that time you've actually spent relaxing."

"It's okay," Maura said, "once we got rid of Bria, I decided that I didn't want to rule, so it was handed off to my brother, who was too scarred from her to make a sane decision, and so he was forced to give it up as well. Maia was next in line because she has governors for parents, but they're too old to rule. I am so glad that I'm not related to her; I would be ashamed."

"You look like you're in a lot of pain from those burns," Lenna said. She coated her hands in water and touched them to Maura's face. Maura sighed. "I've saturated your skin," Lenna explained, "so you shouldn't feel much pain for a little while."

"Thank you," Maura said.

The door to the room creaked open. Gabent, led by Tohphus, stepped in and stared at their prisoners.

"Kill them," Gabent said, and he turned around and faced the door.

Before he could take a step, a bright green light appeared in front of him. A large green ball appeared with green discs spinning around it. When it disappeared, a small girl stood in its place. Gabent was forced to step back. The girl's dark hair was covering her face and sticking out in many places. Her eyes were pink and puffy and she was breathing heavily.

"Vicky?" Lenna asked, quietly.

"THIS IS ALL YOUR FAULT!" she screamed at Gabent. The entire room was filled with a bright green light, and they suddenly appeared back in the throne room. Lenna, Meemee, Rui, Maura, Vesa, and Shenny were released, and they were now standing next to Tohphus. They quickly grabbed his arms and held him down on the ground. "If you hadn't come back, my sister would still be alive right now!" Vicky screamed. The entire castle was trembling as violently as she was. Her eyes began to glow green, and she sliced the air with her hand. Bright green discs shot out at Gabent, making large dents in his armor. The man was thrown backwards, but he quickly recuperated, lifting his fist in the air and bringing it down like a hammer. His spell quickly flew over Vicky and shot down at her head. Her eyes glowed green once again, and she immediately blocked the spell without moving a muscle. Discs appeared around Gabent's body and whirled straight at his torso. One of them hit, breaking his armor off, but the rest went astray, almost hitting the warriors. Without meaning to, Vicky began to tear the ceiling down as well. Large fragments of stone began to fall into the room.

"Vicky, we need to go!" Meemee shouted, running over and pulling the girl up. Rui grabbed her from Meemee and carried her out, and everyone else quickly followed. Gabent and Tohphus chased after them. Tohphus brought forth a long energy rope and shot it at Lenna, who was trailing behind. The rope wrapped around her legs and pulled her back.

"I'LL KILL YOU!" Vicky screamed at the boy, and she pointed over Rui's shoulder and sent out a shot of green energy, breaking the bond holding Lenna and slicing Tohphus' cheek open. Vicky lifted her hand and a green force field appeared around them, moving as they ran. They burst through a doorway and found Divy, Mira, Lisha, and Kita standing in the next room.

"There you are!" Mira said.

"Gabent's coming!" Maura shouted. "Run!"

"What can we do?" Divy asked as they ran down a deserted hallway. "My group, I mean."

"Keep him occupied! If we don't stop him, he'll follow us wherever we go," Meemee said.

"You all go, I'll do it!" Kita ordered, stopping.

"Are you sure?" Divy and Lisha shouted back at the same time.

"Yes, go!" Kita shouted, turning around.

"Okay! Vicky, get us out of here, please!" Lenna pleaded.

"Wait!" Vicky shouted. She opened her palm. *"Dispact!"* A green ball of light shot out of her hand and disappeared through one of the walls. "Okay!"

"Send us to Helite!" Maura ordered.

"Why?" Vicky asked.

"Trust me!" The group disappeared in a swirling green flash of light.

Chapter 10:
Kita's Labyrinth

Kita turned around and faced the empty hallway. The door at the other end burst open, and Gabent and Tohphus came running through. Kita smiled at them and then waved goodbye. She stomped her foot and the stone floor opened up, causing Gabent and Tohphus to fall.

"Here I come!" Kita shouted, and she dove down to the deeper parts of the castle. Flying through the air, she saw Gabent catch himself and begin hovering. Tohphus landed on his back, so she quickly wrapped the stone from the walls around him, concealing him in a tight cage. "It's just me and you," she said to Gabent, landing gracefully.

"I don't have time for this," Gabent said, and he turned around. Nothing happened.

"Oh, that must be the spell that Vicky cast," Kita said. "Looks like you can't teleport out. Excellent!" Laughing, she ran out of the room, pushing walls together at different angles as she ran. Soon she was on the other side of the castle.

"Where did you go?" she heard Gabent's deep voice shout.

"Let's see you try to get out now," she answered. "Here I am!" She opened holes in the walls so that the man was looking directly at her. He jumped up and flew through them, but Kita remained stationary. Gabent was rushing towards her, and as he flew, he watched her take a step forward, bring her arm down in front of her, and then pull it up over her head. Next thing he knew, he wasn't moving anymore. One of the walls had closed on his torso, and Kita just stood there smiling and laughing. "Try to catch me!" she shouted, and she ran into her freshly formed maze.

Kita ran through the castle, moving walls that were already built as well as bringing forth new ones from the floor underneath her. As she ran up one staircase, she heard a loud explosion. "Looks like he's out," she said to herself, and she ran down an empty hallway and entered into a room that she had yet to touch. She knelt down and pounded her fist on the floor. Large cracks appeared from the spot that she hit, and the floor crumbled, dropping large stones to the room below. Kita stared through one of the gaps and saw Gabent staring back at her. She pushed the remainder of the floor down with her feet, but the man simply pushed the obstacles aside.

Gabent roared with anger and hit the wall next to him. The vibrations from his fist sent stones tumbling down from the ceiling one floor above him. Kita looked up but didn't have enough time to slow it down before a rock hit her on her shoulder. All that she heard was a loud crack, and as she tried to move her arm, she found that her shoulder wasn't just broken, it was shattered.

She looked up and saw Gabent hovering over her. Kita stepped back and stumbled over her own feet, falling backwards onto the floor and staring up at the man. He held his hand directly over her face, but before he could hurt her, she rolled out of the way, scooping up a layer of dirt with her good hand and throwing it in his face.

Taking advantage of her foe's temporary blindness, Kita stood up and jumped down one level. Copying Divy's idea, she moved the walls so that it was easy for her to slide to a safe location. When she landed and looked back on her twisted system, she saw Gabent trying to make a getaway through one of the windows.

"Come back here!" she ordered, and she stomped her foot. Five boulders shot in the air and hovered in front of her. She calmly walked up to each one and punched it hard, sending it flying towards the man, who dodged each one and sent them flying back to her. "Really?" she asked, and she spun around and sent them soaring back, making sure to use her good arm the entire time.

"Stop this," Gabent said, rushing towards her. She stood still, as if teasing him, and just as he was reaching out to grab her, she shifted her feet and sank into the floor. Kita popped back up and scooped her hand towards the floor, which jumped up and bent like a spiral staircase. "Come here little girl!"

"I am *not* a little girl!" Kita shouted, running up her staircase. As she ran to the different levels of the castle, she brought down the floors and ceilings so that there was not a single barrier blocking her from utilizing the entire building to her advantage. Gabent chased her as she ran, the collapsing structure slowing him down. "How's this for a little girl?!" she yelled at him, her pride hurt by his remark. She reached the top of her staircase and jumped back down, freefalling to what would seem like her death. As she fell, she broke off pieces of walls and bent them in different directions, adding obstructions to her confusing playground. She turned around and saw the ground coming closer and closer to her. Kita turned her toes to the floor and pointed them directly at the stone below her. When they collided, the stone parted and eased her to a stop.

Kita lay on her back and stared at the ceiling. Gabent slowly hovered over her and opened his hands, releasing a flood of flames. Kita pulled a large boulder from the wall and shot it towards the fire. The rock blocked the flames momentarily, but quickly melted, forcing Kita to raise another boulder as protection. She knew that she couldn't keep this up, for she was becoming too tired having only one arm to use.

Suddenly, a second column of fire shot into the hole. Kita lifted another boulder for protection, and between her outstretched arm and the flames she saw Tohphus standing at the edge of her crater.

"Sir," Tohphus said, "why waste time? Let's leave now!"

"No," Gabent answered, "we need to rid ourselves of this one or deal with her later." Kita's eyes widened at this new danger. She dropped her arm and rolled, opening a gap in the side of the hole which was large enough for her body to fit in. The two boulders smashed after falling from their heightened points, and the flames rushed down to the bottom.

Kita watched as they burned the bottom of the hole, but then they stopped. She quickly rolled over and pushed the ground aside, moving a pathway for her to crawl through. She resurfaced and looked around. The castle was more deformed than she had thought, and she smiled at her work and stood up.

"She's alive!" Tohphus shouted from behind her, and he quickly pointed at her body, a light blue light sparkling on the tip of his finger. Kita jumped to the side in just enough time to dodge his imprisonment spell, and from her new location she repeatedly kicked her legs in front of her, causing large rock spikes to lift up from the floor and pierce a pathway towards her enemies, who quickly floated out of the way. Kita tore a sheet of stone from the floor beneath her with her good arm and bent her body from the right to the left. The sheet rapidly rolled over, forming a tunnel with Gabent and Tohphus in the center.

Kita swung her arm as if tossing an invisible ball, and multiple pieces of earth shot through the tunnel towards the men. Behind them, Kita saw a faint light begin to glow and slowly become brighter. The yellow and red light seemed to fly towards her, and she soon noticed that it was fire which was crawling down her tunnel.

"Who's doing that?" she shouted.

"You didn't think I'd leave you alone, did you? I'm too good of a person," answered a squeaky voice. The flames parted and revealed Lisha standing at the other end of the tunnel.

"Fight back!" Gabent ordered, and he and Tohphus stood back to back and quickly countered the girls' attacks. Gabent floated down the tunnel and stopped attacking. A wide wall appeared behind him, separating Lisha and Tohphus from himself and Kita.

"It's okay!" Kita heard Lisha yell. "You of all people know that I'm a fighter!"

"Okay!" Kita answered. Gabent rushed towards her, hands open and aflame, and reached out for her. Kita reached out to her right and slid her hand over to her left. The wall of the tunnel moved to the left, intercepting Gabent's grasp. He flew around the wall and grabbed Kita's neck.

"What's this?" he asked, shocked. There was a thick brace entirely made of rock suddenly around her neck.

"I moved it up at the last second," Kita answered, separating her fingers and moving the brace, opening Gabent's grip. "Bye!"

she shifted her feet and sank into the floor once again. She moved the earth around her and rushed to the other side of the castle, resurfacing next to Lisha.

"Hello there," Lisha said, firing a burst of flames at Tohphus, who defended himself with an invisible energy shield.

"Hello!" Kita said cheerfully. "Stop that for a minute." Once the flames died down, Kita moved her hands at the entrance of the tunnel, sliding and turning walls so that in the end, Gabent and Tohphus ended up facing each other as well as a whole new path system. The walls were arranged so that several paths were revealed at the same time and the different levels of the castle brought different twists and turns. "Okay, let's run along the top and torture them."

"Excellent idea," Lisha said, and she took off along the top of the walls, shooting flames and building firewalls. Kita insisted on running to the men, waiting for them to fire at her, and sliding a ceiling over them at the last second, causing their spells to hit the newly moved stone instead of her.

"Kita, your arm . . ." Lisha began.

"It's fine, I can't worry about it now," Kita said. She kicked a piece of marble down at Tohphus, who was one level below her.

"You are two of the most annoying girls I have ever met!" Tohphus shouted.

"Indeed!" Kita shouted back happily. She turned around and saw Gabent hovering over one of the lower walls. "Uh oh," she said, seeing the rage in his eyes. The man spread his arms apart, and a large wall of flames spread out across the entire room. The flames crawled forwards towards her, but suddenly parted as Lisha sliced her hand down from an upper level.

"Really?" Lisha asked. "You can't be that stupid." Gabent simply smiled at her and watched as the flames rejoined each other and continued to move.

"Lisha!" Kita called fearfully. Lisha jumped down and moved her hands as if grabbing the flames. She parted her hands and watched as the flames parted as well, but as they moved apart, new ones appeared to fill in the gaps.

"This could be an issue," Lisha said. Kita punched a hole in the ground and jumped down to a lower level, only to find that there was a wall of flames there as well.

"It's covering the entire castle!" she shouted to Lisha.

"What should we do?" Lisha shouted back.

"Surrender," Gabent answered, appearing behind Lisha and putting her in a headlock. The fire-girl struggled, elbowing the man in his stomach and kicking him in the shins, but her efforts were useless.

"Get off of her!" Kita shouted, lifting herself back up one level on a stone. She rushed forward and hit Gabent's leg armor with her open palm. The stone in the armor went flying backwards, bringing him with it, and pushed him up against the wall, forcing him to release Lisha. His arms, legs, and neck were immediately enveloped in the stone from the wall, and Kita held him there as Lisha fought off Tohphus.

"The flames are getting closer," Lisha stated, "we need to go."

"Okay, let's go," Kita said. She grabbed Lisha's arm and opened a crack in the wall, revealing their way out. They stepped out and down a long staircase that Kita lifted for them. "Let everyone else know that we're out."

Chapter 11:
The Elemental Baton

Lenna, Mira, Meemee, Divy, Lisha, Rui, Maura, Vesa, Shenny, and Vicky appeared in the middle of a large forest. To their left was Helite Castle, which was poking its towers over the tops of the trees.

"Okay, we need to go to San," Maura said to Vicky. The group was encircled by a green light and disappeared. They quickly reappeared on the top of a tall sand dune in the middle of a vast desert. Below them was a small village filled with huts built from sticks and rocks. In the center of the town was a small clearing where a large fire blazed. "Let's go," Maura said, leading the group towards the village.

"We should get Vicky out of here," Lenna said to Meemee. "She needs time to recover."

"We need her here, though," Meemee replied.

"Then get her mind off of Ursa," Lenna said.

"Vicky," Meemee asked, "how did you cast those spells? They're new, aren't they?"

"I figured out how to make a new spell, so I made a spell which makes new spells whenever I want them." She spoke very slowly and quietly. As the group walked, Vicky stared at her feet the entire time. "Now I can do whatever I want just by thinking about it. The old spells in the book are useless now."

"That's really smart of you," Meemee said.

"I'll burn that book when I have the chance," Vicky quietly added. Meemee's eyes widened

"Maura," Rui said, "where are we going?"

"Here," Maura answered. They had entered the village and approached a large hut in the center. Maura knocked on the door, and after waiting a moment, a teenage boy answered. The

125

girls' jaws dropped at the sight of the attractive boy, who simply smiled at then in a stunning manner. "Duner!"

"Maura?!" Duner confirmed, shocked to see her. "Si tos iq?"

"Oh, right," she said, turning to her friends. "Duner, like Kit, can't speak your language. Slepa tos si Vicky, Rui, Meemee, Lenna, Shenny, Vesa, Mira, Lisha, te Divy."

"Oh he can speak whatever language he likes," Mira said to Lenna, smiling.

"I agree!" Lenna added.

"You're being disloyal, Lenna," Vicky said quietly. "Chaily's probably watching." Lenna didn't hear her. She and Mira were giggling to each other and watching Maura speak to Duner in his own language. They conversed for a moment and then he opened up a chest off to the side of the shelter. He pulled out a long rod which was exactly as Maura had described back in the castle.

"Lenna," Maura said, "can you come here for a moment?" Lenna happily joined the conversation, standing close to Duner. "Remember how I was telling you about the rod? It's called the Elemental Rod, and it's actually one of five items. We have another one of the items here, and I convinced Duner to let you have it."

"Thank you," Lenna said to the boy, who stared at her with a puzzled face on.

"Im tid'el," Maura translated. "Now, Lenna, you're going to receive the Elemental Baton. It's stored away in a graveyard just outside of the village, so you, Duner, and I will go there and get it. Everyone," she said, turning to the rest of group who were standing off to the side, "you can all go back to Sio. Lenna and I are staying here for a little bit."

"Is there anything we can do to help you?" Vesa said, casually walking next to Duner and staring up at him. The boy smiled uncomfortably and tried to inch away.

"What about Luc?" Vicky whispered. "Have you forgotten him?" Once again, no one heard her.

"No," Lenna said, walking behind Vesa and shoving her back to the group, which was leaving, "we're fine." Vesa grimaced at her. Vicky looked up from her feet and stared at Lenna with dead eyes. There was a loud popping noise, and each member of the group that was leaving disappeared as if they were popping bubbles.

"Maura," Duner said. She looked at him and he held up a finger to her. He stepped into his hut and returned a moment later with a small jar of white cream. He handed it to her.

"For my burns!" Maura exclaimed. "Im tid'el!" She rubbed the cream on her face, arms, and legs and then pocketed the jar.

"Let's go," Lenna said, linking her arm with Duner's and leading him out of the hut. Maura cleared her throat at her and raised an eyebrow. "What?" Lenna asked. "He has another arm; I'm willing to share."

"You talk as if he's not here!" Maura objected, leading them through the village.

"Oh, it's not like he can understand me anyway," she said, putting her head on Duner's shoulder and smiling at him. The boy shrugged and smiled back, enjoying the attention. "Is that the graveyard?" Lenna asked, pointing to a fenced off area on the outskirts of the village which was full of different trees, flowers, and bushes.

"That's it," Maura answered.

"But where are the headstones?"

"Headstones?"

"You know," Lenna explained, "the signs showing where an individual person is buried." Maura laughed at this concept.

"We do things differently here, remember? The place you were buried is indicated by a plant. The richer you were, the rarer the plant your family buries for you."

"So what plant are we looking for?" Lenna asked.

"Is," Duner interrupted, stopping at a small boulder with a single weed sticking out from the top.

"I'm guessing this person wasn't very important?" Lenna commented, comparing the small flower to the larger and more decorated pieces of shrubbery around them."

"Actually," Maura answered, "Duner's grandfather was probably the most important person to ever live on Helite. Few people knew that, however, and he wanted to keep it that way. It was his dying wish that he get one of the most insignificant flowers on the entire continent, and that's just what he got: a weed."

Duner held the Elemental Rod over the boulder and waited. After a moment, the stone split in half and revealed the entrance to an underground tunnel. The boy stepped in first and held his hand out for the two girls to follow. He helped them down and then held the Rod up. A tiny ember ignited from his fingertips and crawled up the staff until it reached the small opening at the top. It sat in there and magnified its light so that the entire area around them was lit up. They walked down the hallway and through an old wooden door at the end. Soon they found themselves standing in a large, circular room decorated with ornate marble ceilings, floors, and walls. Five wooden doors were separated equally around the room.

"Solla so," Duner said, leading the girls to opposite side of the room. Three tiny holes in the shape of a triangle stared at them on a door. Duner inserted the spikes at the top of the Elemental Rod into them, and immediately the holes began to glow bright gold. The door swung open, revealing a thick forest veiled by a thin, misty light.

"This can't all be underground," Lenna remarked.

"That's the genius of it all," Maura returned. "It is."

"Esofos!" Duner called. There was a moment of silence, and then a faint gust of wind blew Lenna's hair. The wind grew stronger, and dark shadows began to move through the trees.

"Maura," Lenna said, "what's happening?"

"Just watch," Maura answered, smiling. Duner stepped forward and looked up to the tops of the trees. The wind grew stronger, and suddenly a large animal burst through the leaves and hovered directly over them. Lenna screamed at the sight of the beast, but Maura and Duner held her arms, preventing her from running. She stared up at the dragon. "Lenna, this is Esofos, Duner's dragon." Esofos screeched at the sight of Lenna and thrust its head directly in front of hers, staring her blankly in the eye.

Duner stepped forward and lifted his hand. Esofos craned his head down and allowed Duner to stroke it. The dragon floated to the ground, coiled the end of its body, sat up, and stared at them, its squinted eyes blinking quickly on the side of his jagged head. Duner whispered to it and the creature quickly began to fly once more. It circled them as if waiting, until finally Duner jumped onto its back.

"Let's go!" Maura shouted, and she pulled Lenna off of her feet as she jumped onto the dragon's back as well. Lenna held on tight as she attempted to adjust herself, but she was pulled up by Maura and Duner before she even had the time to get used to flying.

"Ooh I don't like this! I don't like this at all!" Lenna said, fearfully.

"Well then you really won't like this," Maura said as they soared over the trees and towards a thin beam of light coming from the ceiling. "Here we go!" Maura shouted. Lenna buried her face in her hands and screamed as they flew upwards through a tight hole and burst out into the open sky.

"Tanetnam ey sel riro euo so," Duner shouted over the roaring wind around them.

"What?" Lenna shouted back, her face in her hands.

"He said that you can open your eyes now," Maura answered. Lenna removed her hands and looked around her. They were flying over a large field of dark green grass. On the horizon Lenna could see the faint sparkle of the ocean.

"It's beautiful . . ." she remarked. "Maura, where are we going? You said it was in the graveyard!" she shouted.

"Oh yeah, by graveyard, I meant the ocean," Maura answered. "That's where the Baton is."

"Oh," Lenna said, "so it's on an island?"

"Not quite." Maura stared ahead at the nearing water. Duner, who had his hands on Esofos's neck, steering him, handed her the Elemental Rod. They flew past a series of high cliffs, and then over the ocean. Once they were a good distance from land, Esofos started to dive.

"What's going on?!" Lenna shouted frantically. "Maura! Duner! What are you doing?! Stop this!"

"Calm down and hold on or you'll die!" Maura bluntly ordered. They crashed into the water, and Maura quickly began to wave the Elemental Rod in a circle to her side. The water parted as Esofos continued to dive, and as they plummeted the water behind them rushed past, encasing them in a bubble. Soon Esofos turned, breaking the fall, and flew along the ocean's floor. He turned his head, scanning the sand for whatever he was looking for. He made a sharp right turn. "Hold on tight!" Maura ordered. Duner stretched out his left hand. A large patch of grass burst into the bubble, and Duner pulled a twisted group of blades from the ground and handed them to the Maura, who traded him for the Rod. Maura untangled the grass, dropping what she pulled apart, and revealed from within a long, thin, and sparkling stick. The stick was made entirely from crystal, and both of its ends were sharp and pointed. "Here," Maura shouted over the rush of the water around them, "the Elemental Baton." She held it behind her for Lenna to take. The girl reached out, grasped the Baton, and at the same time released the dragon's back and spiraled into the ocean.

Lenna hardly had enough time to take a breath. She could already feel her body needing air, but she was in such a panic that she couldn't think correctly. She opened her eyes, but the high salt content of the water near Helite made them burn, forcing her to close them once again. All she knew was that she was clutching something cold and smooth, and she had no idea how to use it. Desperate, she pointed it above her and stiffened her body. Lenna was instantly pulled towards the surface of the water, and as she burst through, she opened her eyes and saw a small, black dot floating over the ocean. She blinked, clearing her eyes of the salty water. When she could finally see clearly, the black dot had vanished.

Lenna rapidly kicked her feet in an attempt to stay above the water and examine the Baton. It was a two foot long cylinder with sharp, pointed ends. One inch in diameter, the crystal Baton was sleek and easily handled. Lenna looked up and saw Esofos flying towards her, her companions clutching its back tightly.

"Usually you don't let go of a flying dragon," Maura said to her, reaching down and helping her to climb back onto the animal.

"I didn't mean to!" Lenna responded. "My hands slipped."

"Lenna!" someone shouted. She removed her soaked headband and looked into Ellia's gem. Ellia had a worried look on her face. "Kita did really well with keeping Gabent occupied and Lisha went into the castle and helped her, but Gabent just flew out of the castle and over the ocean. We don't know where he's going."

"Well send someone out to follow him and see what's going on," Lenna answered. "In the mean time, can someone come to Helite and get me and Maura?"

"I'll meet you at Duner's house," said Vicky from her gem.

"Okay see you there," Lenna answered. She put her headband back onto her head and let out a long sigh.

"What is it?" Maura asked.

"I don't want to go back there," Lenna answered.

"Is it because of Ursa?"

"Yeah. I don't know what it's going to be like. Come on, we have to go, though." Esofos took off.

"No ermo sap sia en ej. So sola uo?" Duner asked Maura over the noise of the rushing wind.

"Som erto," Maura answered. "He was just asking where we're going," she told Lenna.

"Oh, okay," Lenna said. They flew over the island, soaring first past the cliffs and then over a thick forest. They abruptly turned right and continued to rush over the trees. "It's getting dark," Lenna shouted to Maura. "Will Esofos be able to see?"

"I hope so," Maura answered, and she watched Lenna's eyes quickly widen in fear. "I'm kidding! Of course!" As the sun set and darkness came, multiple bonfires lit up the ground in the distance, showing them the way back to San. When they landed, Vicky walked up to them with a large plate of food in her hand.

"The people here are nice. They gave me food." Not once did she look up at any of them while speaking, but simply stared at her feet. There was a large crowd of people gathered around the main bonfire cooking their dinners and sharing with each other.

"The good thing about San," Maura said, climbing off of Esofos's back, "is that it's the most secluded village on Helite. The people here have the strongest sense of community, and so they're also the most hospitable."

"That's good," Lenna said, following her, "I just wish they could take Vicky's mind off of Ursa." Up until now, Ursa's death had yet to take its toll on Lenna. The girl had to quickly wipe her eyes in hopes that Vicky wouldn't look up from her plate and see her tears. Maura's eyes had begun to water as well, but she seemed too proud to let it show.

"Here," Vicky said, handing them some of the food from her plate, "eat something, it's really good." Lenna and Maura ravenously ate their food, and as they tasted the different varieties of flavors, they noticed that their moods had been lifted.

"Vicky," said Lenna, "we should be getting back to everyone. Thank you, Duner!" She waved at the boy, who stared for a moment but then waved back, smiling. He walked over to the bonfire and joined his people.

"Okay," Vicky answered. She collected their scraps on her plate and walked over to an old woman who was sitting with her family. The woman smiled as Vicky thanked her for the meal, although Lenna was sure that the woman had no idea what Vicky was saying. "Let's go. *Inimeg fro San portran Circle Stone Room.*" Maura, Lenna, and Vicky disappeared in a series of bright green flashes. They soon reappeared among their friends. Lenna was confused at what she saw. The room was silent, and the warriors were split into three small groups. Grev and Luc were off to the left; Shenny, Ellia, Dimi, Vesa, and Meemee were off to the right; and Mira, Kit, Rui, and Divy were sitting in the center. There was obviously tension between them all. Sensho sat with Lisha and Kita, tending to Kita's broken shoulder.

"Why did you use one of the old spells?" Lenna asked, breaking the silence.

"I have to use the spell if it was already made," Vicky answered.

"Hi everyone!" Maura said.

"Can't we fix it using Vicky's magic?" Kita was complaining.

"Magic can't fix a body," Sensho answered. "A body must learn to heal itself." Hearing this, Vicky silently walked over to Kita and moved Sensho's hands off of her shoulder. She stepped in front of Kita and pointed at her.

"*Cue,*" she said. A green light burst from the tip of her finger and rested on Kita's shoulder. When it died down, Kita began to move her arm again.

"Wow, it's perfect! Thank you!" Vicky walked to her room without responding to Kita. She turned Sensho a cold shoulder as she passed him.

"Who did you send out?" Lenna asked.

"Maia," Ellia answered.

"She's not back yet?" Lenna asked.

"Not yet," Ellia answered, standing up. "Lenna, this is bad, why could Gabent be leaving Sio?"

"I don't know," Lenna answered. She walked to her room and removed her clothes, changing into her sleeping outfit. "Shenny," she said, walking back into the Circle Stone Room and holding up her dirty clothes, "can you wash this for me?"

"No," Shenny responded. There was no argument. Kit stood up and walked to his bedroom. As if waiting for him to lead them, everyone else retired to their respective rooms as well. Lenna watched them all leave and then stormed to Ellia's room.

"What was that?" she asked, angrily.

"Shenny's back, what did you expect?" Ellia replied. "As soon as she walked in, everything turned right back to the way it was before she left."

"Then it's time for everyone to grow up and stop this," Lenna stated. She walked out and went back to her room, passing Vicky and Ursa's room on the way. She peered in and broke out in tears at what she saw.

Vicky was kneeling at Ursa's bed. Ursa's body had yet to be moved, and she was lying on her back with her eyes closed. Vicky was clutching her hand and sobbing into her blanket. She crawled onto the bed and sat next to her sister, her tears dripping onto Ursa's face. She wrapped her arms around Ursa's neck and embraced her. Minutes passed before she finally let go and realized that Lenna was watching her.

"I can't sleep with her here . . ." Vicky began saying. She choked on her tears. ". . . but I don't know where else she should go!" She began wailing, and Lenna rushed in and held her in her arms. They sat on the floor and Vicky cried in Lenna's embrace. Dimi heard what was going on and entered into the room as well. He heard Vicky's problem and carried Ursa out to the Circle Stone. He set her down and then withdrew his knife. Changing it into a shovel, he began to dig a hole in the corner of the room. When it was deep enough, he set Ursa's body down and buried her there. Lenna helped Vicky place a large stone over the grave so everyone would know where Ursa was buried. Vicky stayed there for most of the night, crying into the ground.

*   *   *

Early the next morning a thin portal opened up in the middle of the Circle Stone Room. Maia stepped out, disheveled from a night without sleep, and immediately fell down onto one of the pillows lying on the floor.

"Get everyone," she said to Vicky, who was the only one awake. Vicky clapped her hands and a loud boom resonated throughout the entire area. Everyone sprinted out of their rooms to see where the noise came from.

"Maia's back," Vicky quietly stated.

"He went to Cumber," Maia said. "Any ideas why?"

"That is because I am gone," Rui admitted. "I am the only one on Cumber."

"Then I'm sorry," said Maia, "but your home has been taken."

"Did you see how he did it?" Vicky asked.

"Gabent set something on the top of the mountain and waited. Then some statue grew, and then a castle just like the one here appeared around it."

"It looked like a hand, didn't it?" Dimi asked.

"Yes," Maia answered, "it did. Can I go to sleep now? I was up all night opening portals in the middle of the sky trying to find Gabent for you. I can't even tell you how many times I almost fell out!" Everyone ignored her.

"Vicky," Lenna said, "give me your book." Vicky handed over the book and Lenna opened it up to one of the blank pages in the back. She set it down on the Circle Stone and looked up at the ceiling. "Chaily, I know you're listening. How long do we have?" Everyone was confused, but they gathered around the Circle Stone nonetheless to watch the book. Nothing happened. "Chaily! Tell me!" After a moment, words began to appear.

Two days.

"Thank you!" Lenna shouted. She shut the book and threw it to Vicky. "As of right now, any problems that you all are having with each other are gone! I don't even want to hear about a problem anyone is having with another person. We have two days before the five islands are pulled together and Gabent takes over completely, so the last thing that I want is an issue. Ellia, Meemee, Divy, Vesa, Maura, Rui, get to planning, I'll be there in a minute. Shenny and Grev, apologize to each other and get over yourselves. Sensho, we need supplies. Vicky and Kit, figure out a way to help him with that. Maia, hurry up and sleep. I know that I'm barely making sense right now, but you all can figure it out until I can better explain what's going on. Everyone else, go do something productive that won't be a bother. This is our last chance to beat Gabent before he gets too powerful! We are taking extra charge because now all of you are personally involved in this! We are going to fight Gabent and we are not coming back to sit around and figure out something new like we always do!" As everyone split up in different directions, Lenna casually walked over to the other group leaders and spread out a piece of paper on the table.

"Lenna," Meemee said, "what is going on?"

"In two days, two suns are going to appear in the sky and the five islands are going to come together into one giant continent. Gabent now has two of the five islands under his control, and I'm sure that he's going to try to take the other three. We need to figure out how to prevent this." Lenna looked at Ellia for an answer.

"We're going to need to defend the remaining islands to the best of our abilities," Ellia pointed out.

"Well that's obvious," Divy stated.

"Why don't we just split the groups up again?" Meemee suggested.

"Because it won't be good enough," Ellia answered. "If we split up we'll be outnumbered."

"So then we stall until the islands split up again," Divy said.

"That won't be for a week, though." Lenna said.

"And even if we did stall," Vesa said, "how would we?"

"I don't know," Divy answered.

"But wait," said Meemee, "Gabent's on Cumber right now?"

"Yes," Vesa answered.

"So then who's here in his place?" There was silence.

"Tohphus and Cabe, probably," Lenna said.

"But if it's just the two of them, then we have no problem," Ellia explained. "As long as the islands are separate, Gabent can only be in one place. If we can't figure out what to do about Cumber, at least we can take Sio back."

"And if they call for help?" Meemee asked.

"Vicky will stop them from doing that."

"But what about Cumber?" Rui asked.

"We need to get onto that island afterwards," Maura said.

"How?" Divy asked. "When the islands come together, Gabent's going to see everything that happens everywhere."

"So then we need a distraction," Divy said. "I'll handle that. Mira will do it."

"How?" asked Ellia. "Kita could barely do it, even with Lisha's help."

"So then she'll direct all of us," Divy said. "Me, Kita, and Lisha."

"Who's going where?" Ellia asked, rapidly writing on the paper that Lenna had spread out. Divy read over her shoulder. She had written the headings of two lists, and was looking up, waiting for direction. "Is everyone going into the Sio castle?"

"Yes," Lenna said. Ellia wrote under one of her headings:

Sio Castle:
Everyone

"Our objective?" Ellia asked.

"Completely destroy it," Maura answered.

"Wait, what if there are people in there?" Divy asked.

"Then we'll go in first and find them," Ellia answered, writing quickly.

Sio Castle:
Everyone
-Find people, demolish castle

"Any specifics?" Ellia asked.

"It only takes one person to destroy the castle," Lenna answered. "Vicky will destroy it; everyone else is there simply to keep Tohphus and Cabe out of her way. As for looking for people, we need people who can walk around freely."

"Me and Maia," Maura said. "We'll leave now so we find them sooner."

Sio Castle:
Everyone—stop Tohphus and Cabe
-Find people, demolish castle
Maura and Maia, Vicky

"Okay," Ellia said, "assuming this all goes well, and I'm guessing it won't happen until tomorrow, the next day is when we need to be on Cumber." She pointed to the second heading.

Cumber Castle:
Mira, Divy, Lisha, Kita—distraction

"Where are we going when we get there?" she asked.

"My cave," Rui answered.

"Will we fit?" Maura asked.

"Yes."

"Okay, go now," Ellia said. Maura ran to Maia and informed her of the plan.

"How are we going to do this, though?" Maia asked. "Are we invisible or spirits?" Maura stared at her in silence. "Fine, we're going as spirits. Kit!"

"He can't come with us," Maura objected as Kit walked over to them.

"I know that," Maia said. "Change into a spirit." Maura's body began to morph, her arms expanding into long, black sleeves, and her head twisting around into a dark, hollow hood. Maia stared at the floating cloak before her. "Good." She grabbed the sleeve of the cloak and tore a small piece off. Maura's head immediately twisted out of the hood.

"That's my finger!" she shouted angrily. Her sleeve had changed back into her arm, and blood was dripping from her middle finger.

"Put pressure on it, it'll be fine. And change back into a spirit!" Maia responded. "Kit, good. Make another cloak out of this." She handed the boy the small piece of fabric that she tore from Maura's arm. Kit held the material in his hand as thin purple rings flew around it. Soon it expanded into a full sized cloak just like the one Maura had changed into. He handed it to Maia. "Thank you." She spun around, and as her ponytails whipped through the air, her legs, torso, arms, neck, head, and finally hair disappeared. She donned the cloak and opened up a portal. Maura and Maia stepped in, and the portal snapped shut.

By now, the rest of the warriors had been told what was going to go on and when. They were going to attack the castle in three waves. The first was made up of Lenna, who was the leader, Mira, Kita, Lisha, Divy, Kit, and Vicky. The second was Vesa leading Luc and Rui. Finally, the third was going to be led by Meemee and included Dimi, Grev, Shenny, Vesa, Ellia, and Sensho. The first wave was to make the initial intrusion upon the castle, the second wave was to provide fast attacks from both the land and the air, and the third wave was to act as reinforcements. Once Tohphus and Cabe, along with whatever army they had waiting, were out of the way, Vicky would destroy the castle. Everyone was told to make sure that she was safe.

This plan was repeated during dinner and once again as everyone retired to their bedrooms.

Chapter 12:
Hidden Identities

When Lenna awoke the next morning, she ran through the hallways and woke up her friends. They dressed, washed, ate, and prepared whatever materials they would need for the impending fight. Thanks to Vicky's easy creation of spells, she was able to create a conjuring spell which provided them with whatever materials they needed. This luxury was appreciated most by Sensho, who was able to quickly mix vials of medicine and prepare bandages to treat whatever wounds were caused. Shenny, Grev, Dimi, and Vesa sharpened their weapons and made sure that they wouldn't lose them while they were fighting. Once preparations were complete, the groups walked down the hallway and waited for Lenna to open the exit. The outside was revealed, and the blazing sun blinded them as its light flooded into the dark hallway.

"Vicky," Lenna said, turning to the young girl. Vicky turned to a page in her book and read it quickly. She put her hands together and held them in front of her.

"Intuk," she said, steadily separating her hands. A thin green line appeared from the center of her left palm to her right, and then it expanded and passed over each person in the hall. "We're good."

The first wave walked outside and towards the castle.

"A new spell?" Lisha asked. "I thought you could just make stuff up now."

"When I make a spell it's added to the book," Vicky answered. "Some spells require words and actions; others only require feelings or movements."

"And what exactly did that do?" Lisha asked.

"We're invisible now," Lenna answered. "I thought of it as we were getting ready this morning. We can walk around without being seen from the castle."

"The book knows that I want to destroy it," Vicky whispered, unnoticed. "It won't let me."

"Where's the throne room?" Mira asked. They stopped walking and stared up at the castle. Its walls had been repaired from when Kita had been inside, so there were no openings to show where to go.

"Up there," Lenna answered, pointing one story upwards at six tall, arched windows, "I'm sure of it." Kita bent over and dug her fingers into the dirt, gripping the soil in its place. She breathed heavily and stomped her foot, releasing her breath at the same time. A wide, flat rock jumped up in front of them and floated one foot above the ground. A moment later, a thin column rose up and supported it. Kita stepped up onto the rock, and as she stepped, she repeated the process of breathing, stomping, and releasing her breath. Another rock jumped up, this time floating higher than the first, and was soon supported by another column. As Kita climbed from rock to rock, she lifted others up, creating a staircase for them to scale. Lenna, Lisha, Kit, Mira, Divy, and Vicky followed her. When they arrived at the top, they found Kita resting against the side. "I'm lightheaded."

"That's fine," Kit answered. He examined the wall and found a small crack in it. "Stand back," he told the others. He pointed at the crack and the purple rings shot from his finger. They centered themselves on the crack, and the surrounding area of the wall was soon covered in cracks. The boy kicked down the barrier with ease, and Lenna stepped forward and led the way inside.

They stared at what was once the throne room. To Lenna and Vicky the walls and floor were familiar, but the furniture had been moved around. The marble walls, six windows on the one opposite them, had been untouched, and the dark purple carpeting which covered half of the floor and thinned as it led to a doorway out was exactly the same as well. What was different was a large platform in the center of the room and the lack of a black curtain made to hide Gabent, Tohphus, and Cabe's thrones. Instead of three, there was one throne placed on the new platform. Seated on it was a spirit, and it was staring directly at them.

"Are you sure it can't see us?" Mira whispered to Vicky.

"Positive," Vicky answered.

"They repaired the castle," Kita said. Lenna removed her headband.

"Tell Vesa's group to hold off," Lenna whispered into Ellia's gem. She stared at the spirit. It wasn't moving. Its large hood covered where the person underneath's face would be, and she recalled the first moment she had dealt with a spirit. Just like that time, she couldn't see the emptiness under the hood.

"What should we do?" Divy asked.

"Wait," Lenna said. She continued to stare at the unmoving enemy. Slowly, the spirit stood up, its cloak hovering off the ground. Its sleeve extended out and a small light appeared over its invisible hand. The light floated towards the opening in the wall and weaved between them. Lenna looked at her friends, and then saw how focused Vicky was on the spirit. The spirit put its arm down.

"It can see us," Vicky stated, and she flung her hand towards her allies. Each warrior was encased in a green bubble and disappeared. Instantly, each bubble reappeared in a different spot in the room, and at the same time, the spirit extended its arm out once again, and a large explosion caused the wall above Vicky to shatter.

"Move!" Lenna ordered from across the room, and she opened her hands, stopping the debris from hitting Vicky. "Divy!" she shouted, keeping the rocks from the wall afloat while Vicky ran to a different spot.

"Okay!" Divy answered. He ran forward, swinging his arms around his body and catching and condensing two trails of water vapor. He shot them at the spirit, who disappeared and reappeared across the room in front of Lisha. "Lenna, help me!"

Lisha lifted her arms, and a ring of tall flames began to burn around the spirit. It disappeared once again, this time reappearing closer to Kita, who raised serrated rocks out of the stone floor. The spirit swiftly merged around these obstacles, but wasn't fast enough to see Mira gathering a large amount of air. She released it at the spirit, sending her adversary crashing into one of the stones. Lenna ran forward and shot a stream of water from the air towards the rising opponent. As the stream flew, she closed her hand, freezing her weapon as a single drop connected the stream to the spirit. The water within the spirit froze, and the body of a small boy was revealed. His icy body, transparent hair, and darkened eyes were a shock to all of them. Lenna quickly took her headband off once again.

"Get in here, all of you! It's Ruller!" she shouted to Ellia and Dimi. "Where are Maia and Maura? We need them in here, now!" she shouted to Kit, placing her headband back on. Ruller began to move, his body remaining in its ice form, and he pointed directly at Vicky. The girl was pulled towards him and he placed his hand on her head. Her pupils shrank, and she began to attack Lenna and Mira, who were closest. Mira released another gust of wind, and Vicky, her body being light, was sent tumbling backwards.

"Sorry!" Mira apologized. She turned around and saw Rui flying into the room. "Get Vicky's book!" she ordered.

"What are you planning?" Lenna shouted, running away as Ruller shot explosions at her.

"We need to break the spell!" Mira answered, running the other way. Rui was clutching Vicky's shoulder and holding her in the air as he tried to pull the book from a bag around her back. The remaining warriors were running into the room now. "Sensho!" Mira shouted, catching the book as Rui dropped it. Vicky hit Rui and was released. As she fell, she caught herself in midair and floated close to the ceiling. Ruller was on the floor causing multiple explosions.

"Watch his spells!" Shenny shouted. "Be aware that he can shrink you!"

"Kit, where are Maura and Maia?!" Lenna shouted, panicking.

"Coming!" he answered. "I just called them! They found people and are sending them to Helite!"

"Lenna!" Mira shouted. A loud explosion rang through the room and caused stones to fall from the ceiling. "Protect us!" Mira pulled Sensho close to her and opened Vicky's book. "Help me decipher how to break the possession spell." Vicky swooped over them and shot a trail of flames towards their heads. Lenna quickly swung her Baton and dissipated the flames. She twirled it quickly and swung it down so the tip skimmed the floor. A large stone shot up and bent over Mira and Sensho, batting Vicky away at the same time.

Lenna turned around and stared at the battle before her. Ruller was casting spells faster than ever and Vicky was flying above protecting him from danger. In response, the warriors were focusing all of their attacks on Ruller and none on Vicky.

"Shenny," Lenna called, "trap Vicky!" Lenna twirled the Baton again and threw it up into the air. As it flew, the floor lifted up, following it. Shenny ran up the ramped terrain and threw four knives at Vicky's arms. Two on each sleeve, they pinned her to a nearby wall. Vicky stared at the two girls with an empty gaze. The knives emitted a green glow and moved out of the wall and dropped to the floor. Vicky rushed forward, flames burning from the palms of her hands.

"Luc!" Shenny called, thinking quickly. She held her hands out and the boy threw his shields up to her. As Vicky neared her, Shenny held up the shields and blocked the flames from hitting her. Vicky continued to fly and caught herself before she hit the wall. The small girl turned around and glared at Luc, who was catching his shields from Shenny. She rushed forward at the boy.

"How do we get her back?" Divy asked, joining Mira and Sensho.

"Only Ruller can break the spell," Sensho answered. "We've been trying to figure out how to get him to."

"He's made of water, I can make him," Divy answered, leaving the curved shelter Lenna had made and running over to her. "Give me the Baton." He took the Baton from her hand and held it like a staff. "Keep Vicky occupied so that I can get to Ruller." He ran behind the cloaked boy and stared from a distance. Ellia's many emotions were surrounding him, and Kita was providing protection from any attacks. Everyone else was helping Lenna distract Vicky. "Ellia, move!" The girl absorbed her emotions and Divy stretched out his arms. He closed his hands and pulled them in front of him. Ruller's arms were pulled behind his back and his body was quickly turned around. Divy kept one fist closed tightly and held the Baton in the other. He stepped forward, focused, and touched the baton to Ruller's forehead.

"What're you doing?" Ellia asked, breathing heavily.

"Taking control," Divy answered. He drove the Baton into Ruller's head, the ice cracking as the sharp tip entered.

"What is he doing?" Ellia asked Kita.

"I don't know," Kita responded.

"I told you, I'm controlling Ruller," Divy added. "Mira, what do I need to do to break the spell?"

"Say the word *'hass'* and point at Vicky!" Mira called. Divy removed the Baton and lifted his arms. Ruller mimicked him and pointed at Vicky.

"Hass!" Divy said. Ruller's mouth opened and formed the word, but no sound came out. Despite the silence, Vicky's body glowed violet and her eyes returned to normal. She fell to the floor and was caught by Sensho.

"We have a problem!" said a voice. Maura was stepping out of a portal, now in her normal form. Maia quickly followed. "The spirits are coming up here!"

"Maia," Ellia said, "open a portal to the Dark Lands." Maia quickly opened a new portal and stared at Ellia. Ellia took Ruller's unmoving ice body and pushed it into the portal. It snapped shut.

"Everyone get ready!" Lenna ordered.

"Can't Vicky be here by herself?" Dimi asked. "If spirits are coming, she can stop them."

"That's true," Lenna responded. Immediately, the door to the room burst open and hundreds of spirits flooded inside.

"Everybody get out!" Ellia screamed. Rui flew out of the opening in the wall, leading their friends down the staircase that Kita had made and back to the Circle Stone Room.

"Vicky," Dimi said, "stay here and explode the castle." He turned around to leave, but was blocked by a wall of spirits. Dimi, Vicky, Luc, and Lenna were now surrounded.

"Divy," Lenna shouted, "I need the Baton!" Divy threw the Baton over the spirits and into Lenna's hand. "Luc, throw your shields." Luc threw his shields like discs towards his enemy, and Lenna, swinging the Baton like a bat, created a gust of wind to help them fly faster. Four of the spirits were pushed backwards, and Lenna, followed by Luc and Dimi, left the castle quickly.

"What if the spirits get out?" Mira asked, meeting Lenna on the stairs.

"Help me stop them," Lenna answered. The girls ran to the bottom of the stairs and turned towards the castle. Luc was climbing down and Dimi was trailing behind him. There was a faint scream from within, and then a loud explosion erupted through the roof.

"Vicky's back, where are you?" came Ellia's voice from Lenna's headband.

"Outside the castle with Mira," Lenna answered, removing her headband. "We'll be right there." She put her headband back on again.

"I think that we should help take down those walls," Mira suggested. She extended her hands out and focused on the air in between them. A swirling sphere of air appeared, and she shot it around the left side of the castle and into a large wall, which caved in and crumbled. Without the support from that side, one half of the castle fell.

Lenna held her Baton at its end and twirled it quickly. Four smaller balls of air flew around the right side of the castle, which caved in as well, only slower than Mira's side. Lenna looked at her for approval.

"Ooh, that was good," Mira said.

"It wasn't as strong as yours," Lenna admitted. "You have a lot more experience than I do, though. Given your age, I mean." Mira stared at her.

"I'm only seventeen," Mira said. They walked back to the Circle Stone Room, Lenna embarrassed by thinking that Mira was much older.

"How did I do?" Vicky asked.

"You brought down the entire center of the castle," Mira answered. "In other words, you did very well."

"Did any of the spirts leave?" Dimi asked, almost excitedly.

"Surprisingly, no," Lenna said.

"Oh." He sat down between Divy and Vesa, who stared at him confusedly. "What?"

"Are you feeling okay?" Vesa asked. "You don't look normal."

"I'm fine."

"Maybe Sensho should see if you're okay," Vesa said, beckoning Sensho over.

"I'm fine," Dimi objected, "I'm going to go lay down." He stood up and walked down the Animal Group's hallway.

"That's my room," Luc said, stopping him.

"Oh, right," Dimi said. He walked back into the Circle Stone Room and stared down the many hallways.

"I'll take you to your room," Ellia said. She led Dimi down their hallway and into his room, emerging moments later to join her friends. "Something's definitely wrong with him; maybe he's not feeling well. What do we need for tomorrow?"

"Nothing," Mira answered. "Vicky will send you to Rui's cave and we'll distract Gabent, Cabe, and Tohphus."

"And after that?" Grev asked. "I don't think what we'll do afterwards was established yet."

"We destroy the castle," Rui answered.

"Again?" Grev asked. Everyone stared at him. "This is the third time we'll be running that plan, and so far it's only worked once and that's because no one was there. This time we're all going at them without an idea of what we're doing."

"We're going to fight and we're not coming back until we've won," Lenna answered. "That's it."

"But how will it work?" Grev persisted. "When do we attack? We only have a week, we can't sit there waiting. Gabent's going to take over the other islands as soon as they come together, if not sooner. We need a plan."

"All that we do is sit around and talk about plans!" Lenna stated, exasperated. "For once, can't we just improvise?"

"Improvisation won't work, Lenna," Shenny said. "I agree with Grev, we don't really know what we're doing." There was silence.

"Give me time," Lenna said. She excused herself and went to her room. She laid in her bed for hours, eyes wide open, staring at the ceiling. Eventually she heard Shenny knock on Dimi's door and tell him something. Then Shenny arrived at her door.

"I've finished making dinner, would you like something to eat?" Shenny asked.

"No thank you," Lenna said.

"Are you sure? You should really eat something. It'll help you relax. Lenna, your face has pimples on it."

"I'm just stressed, this is happening too fast."

"This is just like the first time, though," Shenny said, sitting down next to her.

"Yes, but now it's just getting old! I'm ... tired of it! I'm tired of the stress, I'm tired of the repeating process, I'm tired of all this; I just want it to be over!"There was silence.

"I know that you're tired, we're all tired," Shenny began, "but we need to focus on how important this is. If we could, I think that all of us would take a break, but we can't. I think that what you're planning is a good idea, though. Tomorrow will be the last day. You're right; we won't come back defeated again. Now come have something to eat." Shenny stood up and left the room. Lenna rolled out of bed, fixed her hair, and followed.

Everyone at the dinner table was quiet when Lenna sat down. Shenny served them a hearty stew, the smell of which reminded the Circle Stone Group of their beginning days. She had made this for them once.

"The Elemental Group will be more than a distraction, they will be a weapon," Lenna announced. "It's your job to do as much as you can to keep Gabent busy while weakening him at the same time. Vicky, stop him from leaving the castle. The rest of us are going to Rui's cave, and from there we'll decide what we're doing next." She began to eat. No one asked any questions.

After dinner, everyone went to bed.

A shadow was cast in the dim lighting of the Circle Stone Room as someone walked from one hallway to another. It walked into one of the bedrooms, saw an empty bed, and then left to another hallway. Again, there was an empty bed in the room chosen. The person stepped out of the hallway and into the now brightly lit Circle Stone Room. Vesa and Divy were staring him down.

"Looking for us?" Vesa asked angrily, knives in hand. "Go get the others," she whispered to Divy, who quickly disappeared down each hallway.

"Vesa?" Maura asked, emerging from her hallway. "What're you doing?"

"That's not Dimi!" Vesa shouted, pointing at the boy opposite her. She released her knives into the air faster than anyone could see. They hit Dimi in the side, and he collapsed to the floor. His body glowed bright blue, and then shrunk into that of Tohphus. "He tried to hunt me and Divy because he knew that we knew that something was wrong!"

"Vicky, keep him here," Rui said.

"Dispact," said Vicky. A green ball of energy flew from her hand and through the ceiling. She opened her book and turned to a page with fading green text. *"Trescar."* Tohphus was surrounded by a transparent green ball which hovered a foot off of the ground.

"How did you do this?" Meemee asked.

"Isn't it obvious?" interrupted Vesa. "When the spirits came into the room, Tohphus was one of them. He changed into Dimi and captured the real Dimi when he was escaping." She turned to Tohphus. "You need to learn more about the people you're pretending to be."

"Oh believe me," Tohphus responded, "I've learned plenty. Want to know what I learned from your friend?" he asked, pointing to Vicky. "How to create a spell. *Release me!*" He spread his arms apart and touched the side of the ball. It disappeared, dropping him to the floor, his dark robe billowing as he fell. "Wait until Master Gabent hears about this." He disappeared, and the room was filled with panic.

"Okay," Ellia said, stepping forward, "I know that you're all tired but our plans for tomorrow have been moved to right now. Mira, Divy, Lisha, and Kita, get to that castle!" Vicky pointed at them and they disappeared. "Everyone, get together what you need and be ready to leave, because as soon as we can we're going to Cumber. Let's go!" There were quick movements and loud commands shouted as everyone prepared.

Chapter 13:
Three to Paradise

Mira, Divy, Lisha, and Kita appeared in a deserted room in the middle of the castle.

"Meemee," Mira said into the gem on her necklace. Meemee's face appeared in it. "We're in the castle. Stay on here so you know what's going on."

"This way," Kita whispered, opening a door and checking that the coast was clear. It was. They walked down a hallway and through another door, which led them to a circular room with eight stone doors in it.

"This is just like the Sio Castle," Divy stated. He thought back to which door each person on his team had taken when they split up. Vesa's door led to Gabent's throne room. "This way," he said, walking to a door on his right. "Kita, quietly open this, please." Kita slid her hand along the door and it slowly opened up. A long hallway with a dark purple carpet was revealed.

"Let's go," Lisha said. Divy stopped them.

"Wait, you know what I just realized?! Vicky never cast her spell to stop them from teleporting out!" he exclaimed. He looked to Mira for a solution.

"Okay, so here's what we're going to do," Mira said. "You're going to place me a floor above the throne room so that I can see everything that happens," she said, speaking to Kita. "Divy, you're going to lower Lisha over Gabent and Tohphus, and Kita, you're going to pop up through the floor and distract them. Make them think that the spell was cast. Let Lisha know when to hit them with fire." Kita pointed to the ceiling and moved her finger to the side. A small hole opened, and she raised the floor underneath Mira, Divy, and Lisha so that they could climb through. The room they were in was completely dark, so they guessed that they were in an attic. A wide beam of light appeared in the floor, and they knew that it was Kita opening a hole to lower Lisha through. They crawled over to it and stared through.

The throne room below was slightly different from the original one in Sio Castle. The floor was completely carpeted, and Gabent, Cabe, and Tohphus's thrones now sat on a small platform just like Ruller's had. The only aspects that were similar were the white marble walls and the six windows on each side of the room. Tohphus was kneeling on one knee in front of Gabent, bowing.

"They are going to attack tomorrow," he said, "but first they're going to send four of them in here so that we're distracted." Mira looked to the opposite side of the room and saw Kita lifting herself through a hole.

"Hi there!" she said, stealing Gabent's attention. "Remember me?"

"Okay, go now," Mira whispered to Divy. He lifted his hand, pulled water from the air, and wrapped it tightly around Lisha's right wrist. He closed his hand and the water froze.

"Jump down," he whispered.

"What?!" Lisha responded.

"Just do it, you won't fall," he answered, and he pushed her through the hole. He held his hand up in the air, and the ice around Lisha's wrist didn't move from its spot. She hung there and was slowly lowered into the room below.

"You know what's great about magic?" Kita asked. "Creating a spell that can't be broken." She smiled at them and stared directly at Tohphus.

"Tohphus, deal with her." Gabent stood up and disappeared to a different part of the castle with Cabe. Tohphus opened his mouth to cast a spell, but before he could say anything, the water in his mouth froze. Mira and Divy had to muffle their laughter from above, and Lisha dropped a few feet as Divy was distracted. She glared up at him.

"Sorry," he mouthed to her.

Tohphus's eyes widened, staring helplessly for a moment at Kita.

"Now!" Kita shouted, and Lisha forced her left palm down towards Tohphus and shot a jet of fire out at him. The boy jumped out of the way, but his legs were severely burned.

"Go down there," Mira said to Divy, who jumped through the hole and landed in a splash of air-pulled water. Tohphus was drenched. "Okay!" Mira shouted. Tohphus looked up at her, not expecting her to be attacking from that side. "Divy, ice walls! Kita, stone walls! Lisha, keep doing what you're doing!" As Lisha kept Tohphus occupied, Divy and Kita shaped various walls around him, confusing the boy and keeping his eye off of them.

"Stop it!" Tohphus shouted, and he hovered for a moment, contracted his body, and released his energy in a fiery sphere around him. The ice walls melted, the stone walls crumbled, and Lisha's ice band disappeared, causing her to drop to the floor. Divy and Kita were able to protect themselves, but Lisha wasn't so lucky.

"Get her out of there," Mira ordered from above. Kita ran to Lisha's side to help her up, but at that moment, Gabent reappeared in the room.

"Sir . . ." Tohphus started.

"Save it," Gabent answered. He withdrew a small purple ball and threw it at the ground. The ball shattered, releasing a veil of purple gas into the room. Divy turned and darted out the door. Mira stuck her finger down into the room below. Turning it, she moved the air away from her, protecting herself from the mysterious danger. Gabent and Tohphus disappeared.

Mira stared through the hole at Lisha and Kita. Lisha was lying on the ground, unmoving, and Kita was on her knees, desperate for air. The gas traveled into her lungs, constricting and burning them until she couldn't fight anymore. She fell into Lisha's lap. Their hearts stopped.

Mira crawled quickly through the dark room and tried to find an exit. Something creaked below her, and she felt a large wooden hatch underneath her hands. She lifted it and let light blind her eyes for a moment. Mira dropped down into the room below and ran through the nearest door. She was back in the circular room, and she noticed that the door to her right had been smashed through. Water trickled down the side.

"Divy," Mira said to herself. She stepped through the doorway, ran down the revealed hallway, and stepped through the door on the other side. When she entered the next room, she found Divy hiding behind an ice wall which Tohphus was bombarding with various spells.

"Get out!" Divy shouted at her. Tohphus threw one of the purple balls at the floor and disappeared. The room was filled with gas. Mira and Divy ran out of the room and were followed by the gas. Tohphus appeared at the end of the hallway, shot a spell at Divy, and disappeared once again. The boy was sent flying backwards and fell directly into the gas, which absorbed him. Mira watched his profile attempt to stand, falter, and extend one hand out towards her. She was pushed back by the water in her body.

Mira turned and ran as fast as she could down the hallway. She ran through the door, down a flight of stairs, and through three more rooms until she finally came to a locked door. She turned to look behind her. The gas hadn't reached her yet. She held her hands at her right side, focused, and pushed them towards the door. It was sent flying back by the strong gust of air.

"Mira?!" came a voice. Dimi was standing in the next room, encased in a bright blue sphere. Mira stepped in and placed her hands on Dimi's prison. "It's no use," he said, "I can't get out!"

"Hold on," Mira said, sending blasts of air at the sphere. Nothing happened.

"I can't use my gem in here," Dimi stated, "can you get Vicky here to help me?"

"She's coming," said Meemee from Mira's gem. "Mira, you should have let me know what was happening. I can only guess from this point of view. What happened to Kita, Lisha, and Divy?"

"They're dead!" Mira shouted, distressed. "They're dead and it's my fault!" The room glowed bright green for a moment as Vicky appeared.

"I didn't know where to go," she said. She stared at Mira, who had tears running down her face now, and Dimi, who was sad and confused at the same time. "They died. I'm sorry."

"Send Mira back and get me out of here," Dimi said. Vicky pointed at Mira, who disappeared in a wave of green.

"She blames herself for it," Dimi explained.

"Did she kill them?" Vicky asked.

"No."

"Then it's not her fault." Vicky glanced over her shoulder and saw the purple gas floating into the next room. "What is that?"

"That's what killed them, I think!" Dimi answered, frantically. "Get me out of here!"

"Release," Vicky ordered. The sphere vanished. She and Dimi disappeared instantly.

Chapter 14:
The Day of Two Suns

Dimi and Vicky arrived in Rui's cave at the top of the mountain on Cumber.

"Welcome," Vicky said. Dimi stared at his companions, and they stared right back.

"Where's Mira?" he asked.

"She went walking in the forest," Shenny answered. "She said that she needed time to just be alone."

"But Gabent will see her!"

"She can handle herself," Sensho responded. "I pity the spirit that tries to attack her right now."

"Oh, that's right!" Dimi exclaimed. "I found out information about the spirits! Gabent uses water vapor as a base to hold the cloaks up. He needed to do that so that he could see where they were at all times! That's why Lenna and Divy could freeze them!" He paused when he mentioned Divy's name. "Um . . . where's Lenna?"

"When she found out about the deaths," Ellia answered, "she went to Sio." Ellia pointed out of the cave. Dimi turned around and saw a familiar looking landscape off in the distance. There was a series of mountains, and then completely flat terrain with a large pile of debris in the center. Ellia then pointed up into the sky.

"There's only one sun," Dimi said. Ellia walked him out of the cave and pointed in another direction. The second sun was rising past the side of the mountain. Dimi looked around, and turning, saw the familiar forest of Paro. There was nothing separating it from Cumber. As far as he could see, new land had joined onto the island. "When did this happen?"

"A few minutes ago," Ellia answered. "The islands drifted directly over and hit the shore." Dimi turned and stared at the solemn faces in the cave.

"We don't know what to do now," Kit said.

"Can you go find Lenna?" Dimi asked.

"I'll go," Ellia said, "you all stay here. Vicky, can you just send me to the bottom of the mountain? I'm going to walk to Sio." Vicky touched Ellia with her finger, and Ellia disappeared.

*   *   *

Lenna stepped into Lisha's room. Surprisingly, it was full of various books, pillows, and blankets. There were scorch marks on a pile of books in the far corner of the room, and another pile of books was stacked neatly and alphabetized in another corner.

Kita's room was next. Like Lisha's it was full of books, only none of them were scorched and rejected. There were also small weapons lined up next to her bed. Lenna ran her fingertip along one of the larger knives, and a thin slit was made in her skin. She wondered why Kita never showed these to anyone.

Divy's room was last. It was plain and simple, organized with only a bed set up next to the wall with an end table next to it. There was nothing else. Lenna sat on the bed and looked at the contents of the end table. There was one book there. It was thin and well-kept. Lenna opened the book to the first page and began to read. The story began with the legend of Sio, explaining how the original warriors of the Circle Stone Group had stopped Gabent in the first place. The next pages described the night that the new Circle Stone Group arrived at the top of Mount Cris.

"Lenna?" Ellia said, making her presence known. "Are you okay?"

"Look at this book," Lenna said, smiling. "It tells our story! Divy's been writing it down since he came here, and I didn't even know about this!"

"Well of course," Ellia said, "he was always questioning us about how we met. Didn't you notice?"

155

"No, I didn't. I just thought that he was curious." There was silence. "He really was very general about the whole thing," Lenna finally said. She skimmed through the pages. "And his grammar could use some fixing. Look at this, he says, 'Shenny, that just leaves you and I to go to Juff's Beach.' It should say 'you and me'. And he's quoting me with that line, too! My parents would never stand for that!" Lenna was smiling and laughing as she said this, but Ellia stood there, staring at her with a serious expression.

"You're about to cry," Ellia said. Lenna smiled at her, giggled, and then broke down, pushing her face into Divy's pillow.

"This wasn't supposed to happen!" Lenna shouted. "Six! Six people are gone! Chaily, Ruller, Ursa, Divy, Lisha, Kita! Six! Innocent kids were killed because of *us*! *We* went looking for them, *we* convinced them to come here and help us with a situation that wasn't their problem, and look where it's gotten them! We have accomplished nothing! Nothing at all, except having innocent lives be taken away because we were too *stupid* to think out every single possibility that could possibly happen in that castle!" She gasped for breath, tears staining her shirt, and began howling into Divy's pillow.

Ellia sat down on the bed next to her. She took Divy's book from her and looked at various pages. She stopped at one and began to read aloud. "I just want to thank you all for being so brave and for contributing without any complaints. You're each extremely valuable, and I couldn't ask for a better team. So thank you." Lenna stared at her, her eyes and cheeks bright red. "Do you know who said those words?"

"I did," Lenna answered quietly.

"That's right, you did. And you have been given an even better team than before. Each and every one of those warriors waiting back on Cumber had full knowledge that their lives would be in danger if they came, and yet they still chose to fight with us because they saw the approaching danger. You weren't with them, and you couldn't have stopped anything from happening, so don't blame youself for anything bad that has happened."

"But I could've changed the plan so that more people went with them!" Lenna protested.

"And they would have all died too. I think you need to hear something that has been neglected for a while now. Gabent is smarter than us. There it is, plain and simple. With Tohphus on his side he's even more of a threat, and we haven't even seen what Cabe can do. I don't think anyone has really realized what's going on here. We are in a war with a power that can do everything we can with the snap of his fingers and still have time to relax and enjoy the rest of his day. He's distant, rarely seen, and when we do face him, he doesn't seem as formidable as he actually is, but there's no doubt that he can and will kill us all if he has the chance. Our job is to outsmart him."

"But we can't do that! We're running out of people!"

"And we will make do with what we have!" Ellia persisted, almost angrily. "Come on, we need to go back to Cumber." She stood up, held Lenna's hand, and helped her to stand as well.

"What should we do with the book?" Lenna asked. Ellia picked it up and handed it to her.

"Bring it. Use it as a reminder of how far we've come from the beginning when we had no idea what was going on." Ellia looked at an indigo gem on her sleeve and rubbed her finger across it. "Vicky, can you come get us, please?" Vicky appeared between them in a burst of green light. They were instantly gone in another flash.

Ellia, Vicky, and Lenna returned to Rui's cave and stared at their friends. Lenna's face was still bright red.

"Maia, you're going back to Helite and taking control," Lenna said quietly. "You belong there, please keep everything in order. We'll talk with you later." Maia didn't dare object. She opened up a portal and stepped in. "We'll have a conference with Maia tomorrow. Vesa and Luc, you have another warrior on Paro, correct? Feo? Can one of you go find him?"

"I will," Luc volunteered. He looked at Vicky who sent him away with a pop.

"I hope he can come back soon," Lenna said. "Until tomorrow, I think we all should go to sleep."

Lenna walked over to a corner of the cave and picked up a pillow and blanket that had been brought along. She touched her hand to one of the walls, and without any effort formed five hallways that led to enough rooms for everyone. She stepped down one of them, chose her room, and set up the area where she'd be sleeping. She laid down with Divy's book in her arms and shut her eyes. Someone stepped in, covered her with a second blanket, and hugged her for a moment. She didn't open her eyes to find out who it was. Only Vicky could be that small.